# Clinch

## LOW BLOW #1

## CHARITY PARKERSON

--Warning: This book is intended for readers over the age of 18.

❀ Created with Vellum

*Thanks to Loki the Camera Cat for sending me private messages on Facebook by stamping on the keyboard while your momma sleeps. Let your mom, Tian Dreams, know I love her photography.*

*Untitled*

**Clinch— a struggle at close quarters, where fighters become too closely engaged for blows.**

## Chapter One

THE CONSTANT WAVES OF RAIN, falling in sheets and brought on by Hurricane Catherine could only be described as the second great flood. Gunnar had been inching his way home, incapable of seeing a foot in front of his truck, for what felt like hours. A half-mile from his apartment, he considered the merits of throwing his truck in neutral, rolling down his window, and rowing his way home. Although this wasn't an unfamiliar situation in the Keys, Gunnar had seen little of it in the years he'd been living in New Orleans. In the two years he'd been living back in Florida, this was his first hurricane. Gunnar wasn't loving it.

He'd turned his radio down an hour earlier, hoping it would help him see. Instead, the silence had given Gunnar too much time to think. That was never a good thing. Luckily, his apartment came into view, saving him from himself and another of his black moods. Gathering his things, Gunnar braced himself to dart from the vehicle to his front door. Before he could get his truck door open, his gaze landed on a lone figure, soaked to the bone, and sitting on the hood of a car parked next to him. Squinting through the beads streaking his windshield, Gunnar strained to put a face to the idiot who obviously didn't have enough sense to get in out of the rain. The man shifted, giving Gunnar a clearer view of his profile. Recognition dawned. It was his upstairs neighbor, Liam.

For almost two years, Gunnar had called North Gates home. Liam had already been living there when Gunnar moved in. Since then, Gunnar had seen Liam come and go hundreds of times. They'd spoken—maybe—twice. Once, when Gunnar had introduced himself. The second time, it had been unusually hot, and they'd made awkward eye contact. It seemed the perfect time to make an asinine comment on the weather. Afterward, they'd both hastily made their way inside, avoiding any further chitchat.

Gunnar wasn't sure what it was about the man that set him on edge. He was slight of frame with dirty blond hair. The other man was also a good eight inches shorter than Gunnar's six-six frame. He definitely wasn't intimidated by Liam. After all, as a professional boxer, Gunnar wasn't threatened by many people. If anything, he was scared he'd break the man if he touched him. Pushing that stray thought away, Gunnar leapt from the truck, hoping the cool rain would wash away his stupidity. He didn't need a man in his life. Liam glanced his way. Smoky blue eyes, almost unnatural in their coloration, met Gunnar's before looking away once more and reminding Gunnar of the real reason for his discomfort. The man was way too pretty to be a man, and that was a weakness that had already almost destroyed him once in this lifetime. Still, Gunnar couldn't walk away.

"Is everything okay?"

The gorgeous eyes were back, searching Gunnar's face. "I locked my keys in my car."

That sucked. "Is there anyone you can call?"

Liam glanced away, turning his chin to the sky as if praying for the ground to swallow him whole before meeting Gunnar's stare again. "My phone is in my car as well."

In the worst timing ever, a smile pulled at Gunnar's lips. There was nothing funny about Liam's situation, but the man looked so freaking adorable sitting dejected in the pouring rain. Yeah, he was maybe a little twisted.

"Would you like to come in, dry off, and use my phone?"

Liam shrugged, as if it truly didn't matter.

Gunnar snorted. "Did you have a different plan in mind?"

"I'm attempting to work up the fortitude to bust my window out."

With a wink, Gunnar nodded toward his apartment. "Come on. My plan is better."

Obviously recognizing Gunnar was right, Liam slid from the hood of his car and followed on Gunnar's heels. Gunnar was soaked now too. Maybe not as much as Liam, but definitely uncomfortable. The cold blast of air coming from inside the apartment hardened Gunnar's nipples and brought chill bumps to his skin. He couldn't imagine how Liam felt. Liam stopped at the doorway and toed off his shoes, leaving them outside.

One corner of Liam's mouth lifted when he noticed Gunnar watching him. "They're ruined anyhow. No sense in destroying your carpet."

Gunnar shrugged. "I could give a fuck about this carpet, but whatever." After tossing his keys on the coffee table, Gunnar toed off his shoes and pulled his shirt over his head. He fucking hated being wet in his clothes. A sound came from Liam. Gunnar glanced over in question. Liam was looking everywhere but at him. "Did you say something?"

Liam focused on Gunnar. His gaze openly swept over Gunnar's body. For the first time in years, Gunnar fought back the urge to flex. He swallowed down a laugh over the ridiculousness of the situation. There wasn't an ounce of lust showing on Liam's face.

"You have a cat."

Gunnar glanced behind him in time to catch the last wisp of Loki's bushy orange tail zipping in the opposite direction. "Yeah. I fed him once and he wouldn't go away, so I finally gave in and kept him." Okay, so maybe he'd fed the cat several times and liked him a little more than he let on.

Laughter shone in Liam's eyes, but no smile appeared. "I wouldn't have taken you for being a cat person. What's his name?"

"Loki."

This time, Liam smiled. "Like the trickster god. I like it."

Gunnar shook his head. "No. Like he's *low key* crazy as fuck. Unfortunately, the first time I took him to the vet, they spelled it wrong, and he's been Loki ever since."

Liam blinked, looking more than a little confused. "If he's crazy, you should've named him No Chill."

Gunnar didn't miss a beat. "Who the fuck names a cat No Chill?"

"All right."

It took everything Gunnar possessed to bite back the laughter rising in his throat at Liam's response. It was more than obvious he thought Gunnar was insane, but Liam kept it to himself.

Waving for Liam to follow, Gunnar headed for the bedroom. "We're not anything close to the same size, but I'm sure I can find something for you to wear until you can get your keys." He dug around inside his dresser until he found a pair of sweat pants. "These are probably too long, but they're kind of tight on me, and it's the best I can do." Loki was weaving in and out of Liam's legs, leaving fur behind on Liam's wet pants. The sight distracted Gunnar. Not only did Loki never rub on anyone, the expression Liam wore was priceless. The man looked uncomfortable as fuck on every level. Gunnar chose to make it worse because he couldn't stop. "If he scratches you while you're changing, I'm sorry. For some reason, he hates everyone. If it makes you feel any better, I feed him, and he barely tolerates me."

Liam's gaze dropped to Gunnar's mouth for a second. It happened fast enough to make Gunnar question if it had been his imagination. "It won't be the worst thing to happen to me today. I think I'll survive it."

Gunnar passed the sweats Liam's way. "You do seem to be having a pretty shit time of it, but don't worry. I'm good luck. I'll have you back on track in no time."

Liam barely glanced at the material in his hands. "Thank you."

Gunnar smirked. He couldn't help it. It was out of his control. "Think nothing of it. Getting sexy men out of their clothes is sort of my thing." As much as Gunnar wanted to bite of his tongue, he was helpless against Liam's sexiness.

Instead of smiling as Gunnar expected, Liam tilted his head to one side, eyeing Gunnar as if attempting to figure him out. After a moment, he shook his head. "I meant, thank you for letting me dry out."

Giving up, Gunnar headed for the door. "Bring your wet clothes out with you and I'll toss them in the washer or get you a plastic bag. Whatever works for you."

He closed the bedroom door behind him without waiting for Liam's response. Gunnar had learned long ago not to give other people a chance to argue. He liked having his way too much, and if he gave Liam time, he might notice Gunnar hadn't yet given him a shirt. Yep. It was all part of his evil plan. Finding a pair of workout shorts in the dryer, Gunnar quickly stripped and changed into them. He didn't care if Liam caught him bare-assed, but Liam might. As Gunnar tossed his wet clothes inside the washer, Liam reappeared. Gunnar turned and almost swallowed his tongue.

Even with the string pulled tight, Gunnar's pants rode low on Liam's hips. They looked in danger of falling. Gunnar prayed it happened. Every inch of bare skin above the waistband of the sweat pants was covered in ink. Some of it trailed below the waist, and Gunnar had never wanted to follow a line of skull art so badly in his life... with his tongue. The man's nipples were pierced, completing the erotic fantasy building in Gunnar's mind. Try as he might, Gunnar couldn't stop staring. His gaze continued down the path of Liam's body. Were the nipple piercings the only secret jewelry Liam sported or was there more? Gunnar needed to know. One leg of Liam's pants was pushed up to his knee, exposing a tatted leg. Gunnar clenched his back teeth to keep from moaning.

He couldn't remember the last time he'd been this tempted.

When Gunnar met Liam's gaze once more, Liam's lips lifted in a sweet smile before falling back into his usual serene expression. His obvious cluelessness over Gunnar's level of desire only deepened Gunnar's longing. Liam held a bundle of wet clothes. Gunnar snagged them and tossed them in the washer without giving Liam time to ask for a bag. He was seeing this man again. If it took holding Liam's clothes hostage to achieve the goal, Gunnar wasn't above it.

A low chuckle left Liam's lips and brushed over Gunnar's body. Fuck, even the man's laugh was hot as hell. "You didn't have to do that. I could've taken them home."

Gunnar had to swallow past the desire burning in his throat to speak. "Now you don't have to. I left my phone in the living room if you'd like to borrow it."

"Thanks," Liam said, flashing a genuine smile. Fuck. He had dimples. Gunnar was in trouble. Liam turned and lust nearly blasted Gunnar off his feet. The string in the sweat pants wasn't the only thing holding up the material. A perfectly round and firm ass helped. As much as Gunnar wanted to stare all day, the dragon wings tattooed on Liam's back distracted him. Not to mention, Loki still followed on Liam's heels. Gunnar had never seen his wild beast smitten with anyone. He was seeing it now.

LIAM COULD FEEL GUNNAR'S STARE burning a hole between his shoulder blades. He let it go on. It wasn't as if he could stop Gunnar from doing anything he wanted anyhow. Damn. The man's body was freaking amazing. The way his wet shirt had clung to every defined line before Gunnar whipped it over his head was burned into Liam's brain. The man was hardened steel. Everywhere Liam looked,

Gunnar's body was solid. Liam kept curling his hands into fists to keep from reaching over to poke Gunnar in the chest. No one should be so ridiculously perfect. What Liam couldn't figure out was Gunnar's game. They'd passed each other on the way to their cars several times in the past and never really spoken. Now, Gunnar kept eyeing Liam like candy. It didn't make sense. Of course, it was possible Gunnar spoke to everyone the same way. He'd met countless men like Gunnar at the club where Liam worked—a smile on their lips and in their eyes but not in their hearts.

Gunnar snagged his phone from the table and typed in his security code before passing it Liam's way. "Here. I'll make coffee while you call for help."

Liam dipped his chin and accepted Gunnar's phone. "Thank you." Even Liam couldn't figure out why he kept repeating his thanks.

A wicked smile twisted Gunnar's lips and a seductive glint entered his eyes. "Think nothing of it. Just be sure to tell whoever it is there's no hurry. I've got you covered and plan to keep you warm."

Glancing down at the device in his hand, Liam did his best to hide the way Gunnar's claim affected him. "Sure thing." An evil smile grew in Liam's head when he heard the disinterest in his voice. When Gunnar disappeared, Liam dialed one of the few numbers he actually knew by heart. By the fourth ring, worry crawled over his skin. He did not want to be stuck here for any longer than necessary. When the "hello" rang through the line, Liam's knees weakened.

"Hey, Kaz. It's Liam. I need you."

"What's up?"

"I'm a total dumbass. When I got home, I jumped out to see if I had a low tire and locked my keys and phone in my car."

Thankfully, Kaz didn't call him an idiot. "Whose phone are you calling from?"

"My neighbor's."

Kaz made a humming noise in his throat. "Which neighbor?"

Liam drew a deep breath for strength. He knew what would happen next. "The one below me."

A roar of laughter exploded, making Liam's ears ring. Liam talked over the top of Kaz's chuckles, hoping to get out of this with his some of his pride still intact. "Can you bring my spare keys over?"

"Yeah. Give me about half an hour and I'll be there." Even though Liam could still hear the humor in Kaz's tone, he was too damn relieved to call him on it.

"Thanks. I'll keep an eye out for you." As Liam disconnected his call, Gunnar appeared behind him, close enough that Liam could feel the heat rolling off the other man's body.

"Did you find someone?"

Liam slowly turned, measuring his every move and hoping to hide his discomfort. "Yeah. My friend will be here in about thirty minutes. I hope I'm not inconveniencing you."

"Not at all," Gunnar said, sounding as if he meant it. "How do you take your coffee?"

It seemed he was drinking coffee... with Gunnar. "Black."

"Hardcore. Okay, I'll be right back."

Against his will, Liam watched Gunnar walk away. Even the muscles in the man's back were freaking perfect. Liam's mouth watered. He tore his gaze away and headed for the couch. Claws sank into the top of his foot when he took a step.

"Ow. Son-of-a," Liam said under his breath. Glancing down, he noticed Loki spread out between his feet, looking innocent. With a growl, he scooped the cat off the floor. "Damn, crazy.

Hiss or something next time so I know you're there. Sadistic might be your type, but it's not mine." Loki draped over his arm like a limp noodle. Liam rolled his eyes as he settled on the couch with the cat in his lap. "Don't play dead now. It's too late."

Gunnar reappeared with two cups in his hand. His steps faltered when he glanced Liam's way. "Dude, crazy as fuck is actually sitting in your lap. He doesn't let anyone touch him."

Liam scratched Loki behind the ear. "I'm a nice person."

"I don't doubt it," Gunnar agreed, handing over one of the cups and settling in beside Liam on the couch. He took a sip of his coffee before focusing on Liam. "Tell me about all this ink. It's pretty badass."

Heat crawled up Liam's cheeks. He mentally forced it away. "We'd be here all night."

"I've got time."

He eyed Gunnar at the claim. The man looked ready to settle in for a chat. Giving up, Liam shrugged. "I've always been an artist at heart. Rather than becoming a starving artist, as my mom always feared after I got my art degree, I decided to get my designs tattooed on my body. Not all of them, of course, but my favorites."

Gunnar leaned closer, inspecting the tree tattooed on Liam's side. Liam dutifully lifted his arm so Gunnar could get the entire picture. "That's amazing work. If you're not using your art degree, what are you doing?"

No way in hell was Liam answering that question. He wasn't ashamed of his job. It was Gunnar. The man was too much of everything. Liam tried to protect what he could of himself. "I have three degrees. One in art, one in radiology, and another in business. I guess you could say I'm a career student. What about you?"

"I'm a boxer."

Of course he was. "Professionally?"

"Yes." There wasn't an ounce of pride in Gunnar's tone. That surprised Liam.

"Sorry. I don't keep up with sports."

Gunnar took another sip of his coffee and shrugged. "It's a lot of traveling and fighting in dives. Not many fights end up on TV, and most fighters achieve no fame beyond their circles. It's never been about that for me. I've always been a physical person and I don't like to sit still. An office job, or anything I can think of doing other than this, sounds like hell to me."

Liam made a scary discovery. He could listen to Gunnar talk all night. His voice lacked passion, but his eyes didn't. Liam saw the love for his career in Gunnar's gaze. For some reason all his own, Gunnar obviously didn't want anyone to see his pride. Liam wondered how anyone could miss it.

"I get the impression you're very good but don't want to show it."

Gunnar's eyes flashed with wickedness. "I'm very good at a lot of things, and I'd love to show you."

"Do you have a lot of local fights? I'd love to see you at work." Liam wasn't the least bit ashamed of playing dumb. Gunnar was the type of person who would eat him alive. Plus, watching Gunnar blink, trying to decide if Liam was dense or fucking with him, was priceless. Gunnar's expression cleared, making Liam wonder what he'd try next.

"I moved past most of the local bouts a couple of years ago. If you'd like, you can hit the gym with me next time I'm due to spar. It's not the same, but you'd get to check out some of my moves. Unless you'd like to see a few of them right now."

It was getting harder to keep his emotions from showing. Liam flashed Gunnar his most innocent smile. "I've already had my ass kicked by life today. Let's skip literally kicking my ass, okay?"

Gunnar's gaze swept over Liam's body. "You might not be in my weight class, but you're in damn good shape. I think you could hold your own."

Liam could honestly say he'd never been more off-balance in his life. Every time Gunnar switched from hot to sweet, Liam couldn't decide which of them was flirting and who was dodging.

"Are you ready for more coffee?"

"I haven't touched this cup," Liam said, feeling guilty. He'd been engrossed in all things Gunnar. Liam had completely forgotten about the cup in his hand. He brought it to his lips. Even lukewarm, the brew was delicious. It was like there was nothing Gunnar could do wrong. "It's perfect." Liam felt the "goddamn it" at the end was understood, so he kept it to himself.

"Thank you. I can't take credit. It's the ridiculously expensive coffee maker my mom bought for me the Christmas before she passed. I never would've bought it for myself."

"Your mom passed away?" Liam tried reeling in his surprise when he realized he sounded as if he cared too much for a stranger. "That's a tough loss."

Gunnar glanced away and set his cup aside. "Yeah. She'd been fighting cancer for years and was exhausted."

"I'm sorry to hear that."

"Are you close with your family?" Gunnar asked, keeping the conversation moving.

Liam thought over his answer carefully. He didn't want to give himself away. "Yes. I was blessed with amazing parents and I have a younger sister who isn't half bad either."

At his answer, Gunnar smiled. It was sweet and genuine. Liam took it in the chest. Thankfully, a knock landed on the door, saving Liam. He nearly leapt from the couch in his relief. He slowed his steps when he remembered it wasn't his house and it would be rude if he answered Gunnar's door.

"I don't think that was half an hour," Gunnar said, heading for the door. "I feel cheated," he added as he tugged it open. Gunnar blinked at the man standing on the other side. Liam experienced an unwanted spurt of jealousy. They were better matched. Kaz equaled Gunnar in height and outweighed him by fifty pounds of solid muscle. He also had intense jade eyes that were mesmerizing and perfect golden skin, thanks to his Korean father. Not to mention, Kaz had an orgasm-worthy accent due to his English born mother. "Kaz? What brings you here?"

Gunnar already knew Kaz. That was fucking fantastic. Liam didn't know where to start on how that information ranked on the fucking fantastical scale.

"I'm here for Liam."

Stepping back, Gunnar silently invited Kaz in. "Wow. This is a really small world."

"You know each other," Liam said, pointing out the obvious.

"Somewhat," Kaz said at the same time as Gunnar said, "Not really."

"He comes into Merge once in a while," Kaz clarified.

That made Liam feel a little better. Merge was a popular nightclub where Kaz worked as a bouncer. Since both Kaz and Gunnar stood out in a crowd and were each unforgettable in his own right, it made sense they'd met.

Liam nodded. "You're right. It is a small world." Smaller than Gunnar realized. He focused on Gunnar. "Thank you again for helping me. I'll return your clothes as soon as possible."

"No rush. I know where you live."

There was a promise in Gunnar's words some-where, if Liam wasn't mistaken. Liam headed for the door, awkwardly scooching past Gunnar with Kaz on his heels, and attempting not to touch Gunnar as he went. The humor flashing in the other man's gorgeous eyes made Liam wonder if he knew what Liam was about.

"I'll be seeing you soon, neighbor," Gunnar said once Liam cleared the doorway. Liam swore he could feel Kaz laughing at him on the inside. To give his friend credit, he held his tongue until Liam retrieved his keys and phone from the car and was halfway up the stairs.

"Dare I ask what happened to your clothes?"

Liam tossed an annoyed look over his shoulder. "The same thing that happens every time I'm alone with Gunnar. I lost them." Liam turned his attention back to storming up the stairs. "But sure; you, he remembers," he added under his breath.

"Well, yeah. Who could forget me?"

Liam growled.

Kaz chuckled. "Seriously, dude. He sees me at least once a month at Merge. He hasn't seen you in how long?"

"Ten years," Liam admitted as he unlocked his front door.

"Exactly. I didn't know you back then, but I've seen the pics. You look nothing like you used to. Anything," Kaz repeated as if he couldn't stress it enough. "It's not really fair to be mad at him over it."

"I'm not mad," Liam said, only half lying. "It's been a bad day and an awkward evening. You know it takes a lot to make me uncomfortable. I've been uneasy as fuck for the past half hour. It's set my teeth on edge."

Kaz plopped down on the couch, looking thoughtful. "If you ask me, you could use some shaking up. If this man makes you feel anything at all, he's got my vote."

Liam narrowed his eyes at Kaz. "No."

Holding his hands up in surrender, Kaz gave in. "Whatever. You know him. I don't. But," Kaz added, obviously not intending to give it up as easily as Liam hoped, "to be fair, it *has* been ten years. You don't really know him any longer either."

A smile tugged at the corners of Liam's mouth. He'd always been damnably hard to keep down for long. "It doesn't matter. If he's anything like he was back then, he's a people fixer and a good guy. He'd go insane trying to repair all this damage. I don't want that. Not that any of this matters at all. He doesn't remember me. Let's leave it at that. I'll return his clothes, get mine back, and that'll be the end of it."

Kaz nodded, but his smirk said something else entirely. "Sure."

Liam rolled his eyes. "What?"

"I didn't say a word."

"But you thought it," Liam shot back.

It was Kaz's turn to shrug. "Not that what I think counts for shit, but you're pretty fucking unforgettable." The way Kaz said that, and the way his gaze roamed over Liam's body as he made the claim made Liam's chest hurt. It was a cruel game Kaz played. "He's got you in his sights now. It's only a matter of time."

"Fantastic."

Kaz smiled at Liam's dry tone. His expression changed. Liam's stomach dropped. He had a bad feeling he knew exactly where this was headed. Kaz opened his mouth and brought Liam's fears to life.

"You know, when you called today, saying you needed me, an unexpected shot of hope hit me in the chest. I haven't heard you say those words in a long time."

Liam ground his teeth until he feared one might crack. "Don't." He could hear the warning in his tone. There was no way Kaz missed it, but it didn't stop him.

"I've been thinking about you—about us."

"Stop," Liam said, slicing his hand through the air. "I'm still me, and you're still you. Remember?"

Kaz's expression closed. "I'm aware it's all my fault."

With a growl, Liam swiped his hands through his hair, contemplating pulling it out by the roots. "No. It's no one's fault. I just can't do this today. Okay?"

"Fair enough," Kaz said, nodding. His eyes said something different and Liam didn't possess the strength to fix it. Instead, he changed the subject.

"Thanks for coming to my rescue. I won't forget it."

Shifting to his feet, Kaz flashed Liam a sad smile. "I didn't come to your rescue. That was Gunnar. All I did was bring your keys. I'll get out of your hair. It's almost time for me to head to work." Before Liam could step out of his reach, Kaz snagged Liam's waist and pulled him in for a hug. Warmth engulfed him, along with Kaz's familiar scent. Liam's gut twisted as he forced his head still. The desire to turn his face Kaz's way and inhale Kaz's cologne into his lungs was as overwhelming as it was heartbreaking. Kaz didn't release him right away. Instead, he was the one who turned his head and touched his lips to the spot beneath Liam's ear. Liam quickly stepped back.

"Thanks again." Even to his ears, Liam sounded overly bright. The flash of hurt passing over Kaz's features tightened Liam's throat. Sometimes, he thought he could hate Kaz. He had no right to miss Liam two years too late. The invisible weight sitting on Liam's shoulders grew heavier as he followed Kaz to the door.

Kaz flashed a forced smile. "Text me when you get off work tonight, so I know you made it home safely."

"I always do." And that was why Liam never found the strength to hate Kaz. No one else worried about him. With the door locked behind Kaz, Liam set his forehead against the cool wood and let the memories he'd tried hard to forget overcome him.

*He'd never been more nervous in his life. Liam wiped his palms down his jeans for the third time before knocking on the plain white door. Gunnar Hutchinson had lived down the street for as long as Liam could remember. They'd never been a part of the same crowd. Gunnar was athletic in every way. He played every sport and looked the part. Everyone loved him. Liam was small and wore glasses, making everyone assume he was a nerd. In truth, he wasn't that smart either. Liam didn't fit with any crowd. Toss in the fact Liam was gay, and life had been rough to say the least.*

*His parents had taught him to be proud of who he was, no matter what others thought. Unfortunately, what others thought was Liam needed the gay kicked out of him. That is, until today. Today, Gunnar had stepped in. His senior and star football player status had all but one of Liam's tormentors backing down. The final holdout had given in after Gunnar nearly broke the guy's arm. For him. No one had ever stood up for Liam before. He couldn't let that go without giving his thanks. Which brought him back to why he was here, knocking on Gunnar's front door and dying inside from the horror of it.*

*The door swung open, revealing a sleep-tousled Gunnar. His gaze dropped to Liam's feet before slowly returning to meet Liam's stare. Gunnar's eyes were a crazy shade of greenish-blue. Liam* had never noticed before now. He'd always been too scared to look at Gunnar directly. It was a damn good thing, because Liam was looking now, and his body burned. This wasn't good. He clenched his hands into fists to keep from swiping his palms on his jeans once more.

"Um." Yeah, this would be bad. "I wanted to thank you."

Gunnar's mouth lifted in one corner at Liam's dumbass stuttering. With a jerk of his chin, Gunnar motioned Liam inside. Liam went. His feet moved without his brain's permission. The door closed behind them, shutting out the sunlight. It took Liam's eyes a second to adjust to the darkened living room. The house was clean and silent. Liam swore his every indrawn breath sounded like cannon fire. A few open schoolbooks were scattered on the scratched and worn coffee table.

"It's very quiet," Liam said because he couldn't take the silence a second longer.

*Gunnar cleared his throat. It was an oddly sexy sound. "Yeah. It's just my mom and me. She works two jobs, so really, it's just me."*

*They were alone. The uncomfortable feeling scratching at Liam's skin notched up a hair. "Oh." Liam swiped his palms on his jeans again before he could stop himself. Liam's brain screamed for him to look at his surroundings, focus on the beige couch, any-fucking-thing to stop himself from staring at Gunnar's huge frame. He couldn't tear his gaze away.*

*"Why did you do it?" Why had Liam asked? That was the real question. It was as if his mouth had a mind of its own.*

*Thankfully, Gunnar didn't pretend to misunderstand. He shrugged. "I've never liked bullies."*

*Liam scoffed. He couldn't help it. "I have a hard time believing you've ever encountered one."*

"I did today," Gunnar shot back without missing a beat.

"With anything other than your fist," Liam clarified.

Gunnar chuckled. Liam's throat burned with unwanted desire. There was no one less likely to want Liam in return, but his body didn't care.

"You might be surprised what all I've encountered in my life."

Gunnar's claim only served to make Liam's body burn hotter. A slight smile touched Gunnar's full, sexy lips. Gunnar shook his head and released a loud, exasperated-sounding sigh, but his good humor didn't fade. In fact, his smile grew.

"I don't think you realize how you're looking at me right now."

Unfortunately, Liam feared he knew exactly how he was looking at Gunnar. He couldn't stop. "Sorry."

At Liam's apology, Gunnar took a step in his direction. "Are you?"

Since Liam hadn't stopped, it seemed wrong to claim any type of contriteness, but still. He opened his mouth to beg for forgiveness. "No." Fuck. Who was using Liam's tongue to speak?

Gunnar moved closer. "Good. Is it just me, or are we about to kiss?"

"No."

A line appeared between Gunnar's brows. He snorted. "Did you just shoot me down?"

Horror raced through Liam. "What? No. You asked me two different questions, requiring two different answers, so I answered—"

Gunnar's mouth covered his, cutting off Liam's horrified rambling. The breath caught in the back of Liam's throat. He'd been kissed before, but not by anyone like Gunnar, or with Gunnar's skill. Even as their tongues clashed, Gunnar urged Liam toward the couch. Gunnar *eased Liam down onto his back without ever breaking stride. He didn't pull away until he'd settled on top of Liam. Gunnar leaned up. His lips were swollen, and a flush covered his cheeks. Liam's insides twisted at the sexy picture he presented. Gunnar plucked Liam's glasses from his face, making everything a blur.*

*"I don't want to accidentally fuck these up," Gunnar said as he set them aside. His gaze returned to Liam's. Liam couldn't string two words together. Lust clogged everything. All he could do was stare as Gunnar's gaze swept over him before their eyes met and held. "Beautiful," Gunnar whispered before claiming Liam's mouth once more.*

It had been. Liam shook his head, doing his damnedest to shake away the memory of that day. Most likely, Gunnar possessed more skill now, and that was scary as hell, since Gunnar had been damn talented back then. For the life of him, Liam couldn't figure out how he'd ended up back in the same position he'd been in all those years ago—already half obsessed with someone he'd never have. He'd return the man's clothes and be done with him, just as he'd promised Kaz he would.

## Chapter Two

"I'M RETURNING YOUR PANTS."

Gunnar glanced down at the bundle in Liam's hands. When he'd opened the door to find Liam standing on the other side, he hadn't known what to expect. For some reason, this wasn't it.

"Wow. That was fast. Come in." Stepping back, Gunnar waved Liam inside. Damn, Liam looked sexy as hell with the fading light of early evening surrounding him. As Gunnar shut the door behind him, he snuck a peek over his shoulder, hoping to catch a glimpse of the back.

In dry clothes, meant to fit, Liam was amazing. Not as much as he would be nude, but they had to start somewhere. "I'm sorry. Your clothes aren't ready yet. I'm not as productive as you." Gunnar brushed his hand down his bare torso. "Hell, I'm not even fully dressed for the day."

Liam's gaze dropped to Gunnar's chest before quickly returning to Gunnar's face. "No worries. I'm in no hurry. It's not like I don't have other clothes." He set Gunnar's pants on the coffee table, since Gunnar had forgotten to relieve him of them. "I would've called before dropping by, but you know." He shrugged without finishing.

"You don't have my number," Gunnar finished for him. "We should fix that." Without waiting for Liam to deny him, Gunnar scratched his number out on a scrap of paper sitting on his end table. "Here. You'll need this."

Liam took it, but not without question. "I will?"

Gunnar smirked. "Yeah. You definitely will." No one in their right mind could miss the sexual promise dripping from Gunnar's every word.

Stuffing the paper in the front pocket of his jeans, Liam flashed an innocent smile. "You're right. I'm always doing stupid shit like I did yesterday. It might not be a bad idea to have someone close by I can count on. I'd hate for Kaz to have to drive all the way in from Miami just to bring my keys again. Luckily, he was halfway between there and here yesterday, shopping." He moved back toward the door. Gunnar watched it happen. His confusion made him slow to react. Liam baffled the hell out of Gunnar.

He chose a more direct approach since hinting obviously wasn't working. "Of course, I'm here if you need a dry place again, but I'm even better at giving a wet place. I'd love for you to use my number for other reasons as well.

Preferably for naughty pics. Yeah, I wouldn't turn those down."

"Oh," Liam said, smiling. "I love those memes people post on Facebook. I'll see if I can find something good for you."

This was ridiculous. He had to know if Liam was fucking with him or genuinely uninterested. Gunnar didn't think he was conceited or anything. Maybe he was. A little. Fuck, he worked hard on his body and tried to always be confident. People liked confident men, right? Something seemed wrong about Liam's reaction to Gunnar's every attempt at flirting with him. He focused on the vent in the ceiling above Liam's head.

"Damn. What's up with that vent? I keep opening it, and it keeps closing itself somehow." Without giving Liam time to answer or figure out what he was talking about, Gunnar crowded Liam's space, reaching above the other man's head. He didn't stop until barely an inch separated them, leaving Liam nowhere to go. Attempting to make his story look good, Gunnar toyed with the vent, opening it all the way and thanking God for the low ceilings in his apartment. He'd have to fix the vent later or it would be hotter than hell in his bedroom, but it was worth it if he could force Liam's hand.

Without moving away, Gunnar glanced down. Liam was craning his neck in an obvious attempt at inspecting the problem. His expression hadn't changed in the least. But goddamn, his blue eyes were even more amazing up close. They were an odd shade of smoky blue.

"Something probably needs to be tightened." Liam's hands came to rest on Gunnar's sides, as if the man had braced himself to see around Gunnar's large frame and get at the problem. Nothing separated them. It was skin-on-skin, and Gunnar went hard at the sensation. He couldn't stop staring at Liam's face. Liam finally focused on Gunnar. The corners of his mouth lifted in a sweet smile before falling.

Liam shrugged. "Really. I'm just talking out of my ass. I know nothing about heat and air ventilation."

Gunnar tried clinging to a brain cell. It didn't happen. The words fell from his lips without his permission. "Wow. You really are clueless, aren't you?"

Liam opened his mouth. Gunnar could see him gearing up to argue. Without giving Liam a chance, Gunnar lowered his head and covered Liam's mouth with his. He'd meant to make a point. That was all. In all honesty, he expected Liam to shove him away or knee him in the balls. Instead, Liam's tongue touched his. Gunnar's mind went blank. He moved an inch closer, intent on deepening their kiss. Liam snagged the back of Gunnar's hair, beating him to the punch. Gunnar's bottom lip stung as Liam's teeth sank into it. He wanted the moment to last forever. The instant that thought hit, Gunnar pulled away. He already knew what his life lacked. The last thing

Gunnar needed was another fantasy he couldn't keep.

Liam didn't miss a beat. "As much as I want to tell you how it isn't nice to call someone clueless, I'm too curious to know why you'd say that."

The confusion written on Liam's face made Gunnar want to growl. Even now, after that hot-as-hell kiss, Liam didn't seem to realize how he affected Gunnar. Gunnar pried Liam's fingers from his hair before dragging Liam's hand down his body, until Liam's fingers shaped Gunnar's erection.

"Because you do this to me, and you don't even know it."

Liam held Gunnar's stare, boldly stroking Gunnar's cock through his jeans. "I've lived above you for almost two years, and you've never noticed me before now. Seems to me you're the one who doesn't have a clue, Gunnar Hutchinson." Pulling away, Liam took a step back. "Thanks again for the dry clothes."

Gunnar stared at the spot where Liam had been for ten minutes after the man disappeared. He'd called him Gunnar Hutchinson. That hadn't been Gunnar's last name since he turned seventeen. How had Liam known? With no real plan in mind, Gunnar went after Liam. He had to know. It would drive him insane if he didn't. He took the stairs two at a time before knocking on Liam's door with more force than intended. Liam smiled when he answered as if he hadn't stormed away ten minutes ago.

Gunnar skipped the niceties. "You called me Hutchinson. My name legally changed to Samson when I was seventeen."

"Okay."

Gunnar held his tongue for a full minute, expecting Liam would say more. When he didn't, Gunnar barely stopped himself from stamping his foot. "My dad decided he was tired of paying child support, and he'd almost gotten me grown, so he signed away his rights to avoid another year of it. In retaliation, I changed my last name to my mom's. She'd done all the real work anyhow." No one knew that other than Gunnar's mom, and she'd passed away after losing a three-year-long battle with cancer two years earlier.

"All right," Liam said as if awaiting Gunnar's point.

Goddamn, he was maddening. There was no way Liam didn't understand what Gunnar was getting at, but he didn't volunteer an inch. Gunnar made an impatient gesture. "So no one knows that. How did you?"

"I didn't. You just told me."

Gunnar scrubbed his hand across his face. "Jesus. Seriously? How did you know my last name used to be Hutchinson?"

Liam's eyebrows rose. "That seems a bit self-explanatory, don't you think? I knew you before you changed your name. If you don't mind, I have to get ready for work."

Gunnar mutely nodded. His brain scrambled for any memory of Liam, coming up empty. Liam shut the door in his face. Gunnar stared at the wooden surface in surprise. What the fuck? He banged on the door. This time, Liam appeared put out as he answered. He didn't exactly sigh, but Gunnar gathered it was understood.

"Did you need something else?"

Did he? Considering Liam had lived above him for almost two years, and Gunnar had never once recognized him, while Liam obviously had recognized Gunnar, made Gunnar feel like a total dick for not figuring this out on his own.

"Where do you work?"

"No offense, but it's none of your business."

"Fair enough," Gunnar said with a shrug. "Have a good night at work." Snagging the front of Liam's shirt, Gunnar towed him forward and covered the man's mouth with his once more. Maybe he couldn't remember Liam nor could he deny he hadn't noticed the man before the other day. Now he had, and Gunnar would figure out this mystery. Until then, Gunnar needed Liam to understand— he was on a mission to have him. Gunnar kept their kiss slow and deliberate. He made Liam a thousand promises with his tongue. When it was over, Liam didn't appear the least bit unaffected. For the first time, he looked as turned on as Gunnar felt.

Gunnar wiped the moisture from Liam's bottom lip. "Like I said, have a good night at work. Maybe I could see you later."

Liam gave a jerky nod and took a step back. Gunnar let it happen. Dropping his gaze to Liam's bare feet, Gunnar slowly moved up Liam's body, focusing on all the best places before meeting the other man's stare once more. The heat blasting him from Liam's sexy blue eyes had Gunnar's stomach muscles tightening in anticipation. The memory slammed into him. That heated stare. Those smoky eyes. He knew exactly who this man was. Taking a step forward, Gunnar claimed Liam's mouth again. He couldn't stop himself. The mixture of old desires and new hunger had him ready to devour his prey, but he'd learned a little patience since the last time they'd been in this position all those years ago. Gunnar sucked on Liam's tongue, letting him know how it would be before pulling away.

"I'll be seeing you again real soon, Liam Marshall. Of that, you can be sure."

Without waiting for Liam's reaction, Gunnar turned and jogged down the stairs. He needed a cold shower before he snapped.

GUNNAR LASTED ALL OF TWO HOURS before deciding he couldn't take anymore. It was obvious Kaz and Liam were close. After all, people didn't pass out keys to their car and apartment to just anyone on their friends list. That meant, if anyone knew the answers to Gunnar's many questions, Kaz would. Pointing his truck in Merge's direction, Gunnar hoped Kaz would be working. In the past two years, since Gunnar had been back living in Key Largo, he hadn't been to Merge when Kaz wasn't working, but since it was important, tonight could go either way. He also hated the thought of driving an hour into Miami for no reason.

Finding a parking space on a Saturday night turned out to be a huge pain in the ass. It had been a few months since the last time Gunnar had been here. The club was obviously getting more popular by the day. The windows were blacked out, protecting the dancing patrons from the view of motorists passing by. Unfortunately, they also kept Gunnar from seeing if Kaz was working without going inside. The line was ridiculous. Gunnar had three phone numbers he didn't want before making it to the door.

Fortunately, Kaz—like Gunnar—stood almost a foot taller than most people, making him easy to spot the second Gunnar cleared the door. The packed-like-sardines situation made the trek to his side take almost ten minutes. Kaz's eyebrows rose when he caught sight of Gunnar.

He leaned in, yelling to be heard over the crowd. "Admit it. Seeing me yesterday afternoon reminded you to visit more often."

"Not like this," Gunnar said with a chuckle. "This crowd is fucking ridiculous."

Kaz cast a glance around as if just now noticing. "Yeah. I guess things have changed a little since the last time I saw you. Apparently, some famous YouTuber mentioned us during one of his weekly rants and put us on the map. Now,

I'm lucky to make it out of here with my junk still attached every night. So, if you're not here to enjoy my gloriousness, what brings you in tonight?"

"I'm looking for Liam."

Something dark crossed Kaz's features before his expression cleared. "He's working."

Gunnar nodded. "I know. When I saw him a couple of hours ago, he said he was headed to work. That's where you come in. Where's he work?"

Kaz glanced left and then right before snagging Gunnar's arm and heading for the door. Gunnar let it go on. He hoped Kaz was tired of yelling over the crowd and not trying to manhandle him. Gunnar wasn't known for his tolerance. When they finally hit the pavement outside, Kaz turned on him, his fury evident.

"Why are you looking for Liam? From what I gather, you had your shot years ago."

So Kaz knew about that. Awkward. "I did," Gunnar admitted. "We were both teenagers back then. I hardly think it's relevant now."

"Of course you'd think that. You're obviously the type of person who's used to getting what you want with ease. Liam isn't that person. He's had to struggle for everything his whole life. Now, here you are, ten years later. Are you looking to score and move on again? If so, you can go fuck yourself, because you're not getting shit from me."

Gunnar felt his features tighten. "I'm giving you one free pass because you don't know me, but I don't usually stand for insults. Have you ever seen me leave this club with anyone?"

Kaz didn't back down. "Don't think for one second I'm scared to challenge you, especially when it comes to Liam. As for your question, I haven't, but I also don't make it my business."

"That's because I don't play," Gunnar said, attempting to diffuse the situation. He could tell

Kaz meant well. It was equally obvious Kaz wouldn't give up the info Gunnar needed as long as they continued down this path. "I'm not saying I've always been the best person in the world, but I'm better than the man who didn't raise me. If I'm with someone, I'm with someone."

The muscle in Kaz's jaw hadn't stopped ticking, but he gave Gunnar a sharp nod. "You're standing about three doors down from him. Liam works at Fusion X."

Gunnar kept his features blank by force of will alone. Fusion X was a well-known strip club. That was interesting.

---

*THE FAMILIAR FIGURE LEANING AGAINST HIS car had Liam's feet slowing. He'd somewhat come to terms with being a onetime fling for Gunnar. Liam wondered if his heart would* withstand the too-sexy man twice. It seemed he would find out soon enough.

"You work in a bookstore," Gunnar said the second Liam was within earshot.

In spite of his confusion over Gunnar's presence, Liam's smile didn't seem to care. It pulled at the corners of his mouth. "Beats the hell out of fast food."

Gunnar pushed away from the car. "True." He met Liam halfway.

Liam rubbed the back of his neck, unsure of himself. "So, it's been a few weeks." He wanted to bite off his tongue. Even though he'd somehow managed to sound as if the passage of time with no word didn't matter, he didn't want Gunnar to know it bothered him. Gunnar snagged Liam's belt loops and tugged him closer. Liam went. The wicked smile hovering on Gunnar's lips was too appealing to resist.

"I missed doing this," Gunnar said, closing the final inches between them and taking Liam's bottom lip between his. The questions that had been sitting on Liam's chest, suffocating him, disappeared as Gunnar's tongue touched his. His fingers ached, making Liam realize how tightly he gripped Gunnar's t-shirt, attempting to keep him held in place. It sucked, knowing he could become addicted to this. Gunnar's tongue brushed the roof of Liam's mouth, forcing him to chase after it, but Gunnar didn't give in. Keeping his forehead pressed to Liam's, Gunnar backed away an inch.

"Do you need to be home by a certain time?"

"Not on the weekends," Liam answered, willing to see where this was headed.

Gunnar lips touched Liam's briefly once more, as if he couldn't resist. It did something to Liam's chest. "There's this quiet spot by Crocodile Lake. Would you go with me?"

*Liam's heart sank. Gunnar's offer was a blast of cold air over Liam's skin. He knew all the town's hot spots, and the lake wasn't one. Liam hadn't been invited to any of them. It hurt knowing Gunnar was no different. Because he couldn't go without touching Gunnar once more, Liam swiped his thumb across the same bottom lip ensnaring his gaze. The bitter smile tugging at Liam's lips was out of his control.*

*"I didn't get my ass handed to me every day for the past three years to let someone keep me a secret."*

*Gunnar opened his mouth. His expression made it clear he meant to argue.*

*Liam cut him off. "Maybe that's not your intention tonight, but it will be next weekend, or the weekend after that. I'd rather get a little hurt tonight than a lot in a few weeks."*

*His respect for Gunnar went up a notch when he didn't deny Liam's claim. "Maybe I could still call you sometime."*

*Liam took a step back. "You could, but maybe you won't." As Liam climbed inside his car, he resigned himself to the fact that call would never come.*

He'd been right. Funny how after all these years that still hurt a little. Now, Gunnar had recognized him. Liam's cheeks burned. No amount of time could wash away Liam's humiliation. He'd been easy for Gunnar, willing to do whatever Gunnar wanted. It had been so fucking worth it. Liam didn't regret a damn thing.

"How about a lap dance?"

Every muscle in Liam's body tensed as Gunnar's familiar voice brushed Liam's ear. He didn't turn. "No."

"Seriously?" Gunnar asked as his hands landed on Liam's hips, holding him in place. "What would something like that run me? Fifty bucks?"

"No," Liam repeated, moving from Gunnar's light grasp.

Gunnar matched Liam step for step, refusing to back away. "How about later, then? You can dance for me in private. Back at my place."

Liam growled. The sound escaped before he could stop it. "For fuck's sake." Snagging Gunnar's hand, he tugged the man toward one of the private rooms. Finding it empty, he urged Gunnar into the chair. He bit back a moan at the lust shining in Gunnar's eyes.

"Sit on your hands."

Gunnar's eyebrows rose. "Fifty bucks and I have to sit on my hands?"

Liam leaned in, bracing his palms on the wooden back of the chair on either side of Gunnar's head. He held himself away from Gunnar just enough where their bodies wouldn't touch, but he could still feel the heat radiating from Gunnar's skin. He touched his lips to Gunnar's ear as he rolled his hips to the beat of the music playing in the background.

"You're buying a dance, Gunnar. I'm not for sale. Sit on your hands."

THE SEDUCTIVE NOTE TO LIAM'S VOICE HAD Gunnar sitting on his hands. He was scared Liam might stop if he didn't. Gunnar could honestly say he'd never been fucked in his clothes before. He'd been through many fumbling make-out sessions in his life, but Gunnar had never experienced what Liam did to him now. The strength he showed holding himself the perfect distance from Gunnar's body explained the gorgeous sleek muscles Liam sported. His body moved in perfect time with the music. It was mesmerizing. While he was aware of each move Liam made, Gunnar couldn't stop staring at Liam's face. His eyes were hooded. Every few seconds, he'd bite his lip. Gunnar's dick had never been harder.

Liam wore only a pair of jeans, unbuttoned at the waist. He didn't remove them. He didn't need to. Gunnar was hooked. The song ended. Another one rolled in directly behind it. Liam changed angles, coming at Liam from a different direction. Gunnar's gaze followed. He didn't want to miss anything. Liam smirked.

"This could get expensive quick."

"You're worth it," Gunnar said, meaning nothing more in his life. Without his permission, Gunnar's fingertips skimmed Liam's ribs. He hadn't realized he wasn't sitting on his hands any longer until the second he touched Liam.

"You're not sitting on your hands."

And he had no intention of doing so again. "Come to me when you get off tonight."

Liam bit his lip again. Gunnar swore he could taste it. "I don't get off until two in the morning."

"I'll be up. How much do I owe you?" Gunnar needed to get the hell out before he fucked Liam right there.

Liam leaned closer until his shoulder touched Gunnar's chest and his lips brushed Gunnar's ear. "I told you, I'm not for sale. See you in a few." Without a backward glance, he walked away, leaving Gunnar hard as a rock and glued to his chair. As he looked on, a red-haired woman snagged Liam's arm, pulling him to a stop. He smiled down at her as if genuinely happy to be at her service. After a minute of having their heads together, Liam tucked the woman against his side and smiled bright for their selfie.

Gunnar still had a hard time believing Liam, *his Liam*, had grown up and become a stripper. Liam hadn't exactly been shy in high school, but neither had he been outgoing. This shit took guts. Why were there so many women in this club? Gunnar tried hard to concentrate on any detail other than his dick and its begging. Obviously, women went to see male strippers, but on this side of town, it struck Gunnar as odd—not that he hung out in places such as these. He'd always thought he had better things to spend his money on, but now—wow. Gunnar would willingly hand all his money to Liam if only he'd come back and finish the job. With a forlorn sigh, Gunnar shifted to his feet and headed for the door. He did his best not to look for Liam as he went. He'd see the sexy stripper soon enough, and then, Liam would be the one with his hands bound.

---

WHEN GUNNAR HEARD THE CAR PULL UP, he peeked through the blinds. As he looked on, Liam climbed from his car. Gunnar's stomach muscles tightened. He was so sexy. No one should be as gorgeous as Liam. For a full minute, Liam stared at Gunnar's front door. The first hint of doubt settled in. It was too dark to see Liam's expression, but he could practically feel the other man's doubt. He took a step in Gunnar's direction before quickly changing course. He was up the stairs and out of sight before Gunnar had time to decide how he felt about it. He settled back down on the couch, telling himself lies. Maybe Liam wanted a shower after working all night. He could still show up. Gunnar wasn't much on lying to himself. Liam's hesitation had said it all. He was standing Gunnar up. Huh. Now Liam was beginning to feel real familiar to Gunnar.

*The knock landed just as Gunnar dozed off. With a growl, he pushed to his feet and stumbled for the door. His mom worked until midnight and had a key. Otherwise, Gunnar couldn't think of anyone who'd stop by without calling first. He pulled open the door and froze. Liam Marshall stood on the other side, looking unsure of himself. Since Liam was a junior and opposite of Gunnar in every way, they'd never hung out, but Gunnar knew him. Not only had they lived down the street from one another for years, Liam stood out from the crowd. Mostly, it was due to the constant torment Liam endured from a majority of the student body. For Gunnar, there were other reasons as well.*

*Gunnar dropped his gaze to Liam's spotless sneakers before slowly inspecting his perfectly pressed pants and plain T-shirt. When he met Liam's gaze, Gunnar bit the inside of his cheek. Liam's wire framed glasses did little to hide the way Liam's smoky blue eyes blazed with interest.*

*"Um," Liam said, sounding unsure of his welcome. "I wanted to thank you."*

*A smirk pulled at Gunnar's mouth at Liam's adorable gratitude. As far as Gunnar was concerned, he had done nothing special. He also believed Liam should be kicking Gunnar in the balls for holding his silence before today. It was no secret everyone bullied Liam over being gay. Gunnar could've and should've put a stop to it sooner. The reason he hadn't was entirely his own. With a jerk of his chin, Gunnar invited Liam inside. Liam surprised him by accepting without argument.*

*As Liam moved past him, Gunnar drew the scent of Liam's cologne into his lungs. With the door shut, closing them away from the world, Gunnar turned the lock as Liam glanced around at his surroundings. Gunnar wondered what Liam thought. No doubt, he was accustomed to having nicer things. Not that Gunnar cared. He wasn't ashamed of what he had. His mom worked twice as hard as any other parent to ensure Gunnar had the things he needed.*

*"It's very quiet," Liam said, giving Gunnar his first insight into his thoughts.*

*Gunnar cleared his throat, hoping Liam wouldn't run away once he learned they were* alone. "Yeah. It's just my mom and me. She works two jobs, so really, it's just me."

"Oh." Liam swiped his hands down his thighs, looking uncomfortable, but his gaze never wavered from Gunnar's. "Why did you do it?"

Gunnar shouldn't have been surprised by Liam's question. Liam was the most courageous person Gunnar had ever encountered. He always held his head high. Gunnar respected the hell out of him.

"I've never liked bullies."

Liam scoffed. "I have a hard time believing you've ever encountered one."

"I did today," Gunnar said, reminding Liam of why they were having this conversation.

Liam's dimples made an appearance, making Gunnar's mouth go dry. "With anything other than your fist," Liam said, surprising a chuckle from Gunnar.

"You might be surprised what all I've encountered in my life."

Liam bit his bottom lip, pulling a knowing smile from Gunnar. Gunnar shook his head and released a loud sigh, wondering how he'd ended up in this position. "I don't think you realize how you're looking at me right now."

Liam's expression became hotter, making Gunnar want to groan.

"Sorry."

Funny, Liam didn't sound sorry at all. "Are you?"

Liam gained another ounce of Gunnar's respect by being honest. "No."

Gunnar took a step in Liam's direction. It was out of his control. Liam looked game for anything Gunnar had in mind. It was hypnotizing. Gunnar's gaze locked on Liam's mouth. Liam's tongue shot out, wetting his bottom lip. The question escaped before Gunnar could stop it.

"Is it just me, or are we about to kiss?"

"No."

Liam's immediate denial was a blast of cold water to the face. It surprised a snort from Gunnar. "Did you just shoot me down?"

A line appeared between Liam's brows. "What? No. You asked me two different questions, requiring two different answers, so I answered —"

Liam's nervous rambling might've gone on all night if Gunnar didn't put a stop to it. He closed the distance between them and captured Liam's mouth, cutting off his explanation. His lips parted at Gunnar's insistence. When their tongues met, Gunnar's patience snapped.

He urged Liam back, toward the couch. Liam went willingly. Even as Gunnar eased Liam down onto his back and settled on top of him, Liam let it happen. Gunnar's mind raced. His body burned. Yeah, he'd noticed Liam hundreds of times and wished he could be as free. He'd *also noticed Liam's gorgeous eyes, lips, and smile. Gunnar wanted to crow in satisfaction when he felt Liam's erection grow between them. Even though he'd been confident Liam wanted him too, Gunnar had still been nervous as hell he might be wrong. Now that he had Liam beneath him, Gunnar didn't plan to stop.*

*Leaning up, he plucked Liam's glasses from his face. "I don't want to accidentally fuck these up," Gunnar said as he set them aside. When he met Liam's gaze once more, Gunnar's cock leaked at the lust staring back at him. The picture Liam presented was the most gorgeous thing Gunnar had ever seen.*

*"Beautiful," Gunnar whispered before claiming Liam's mouth once more.*

He'd meant nothing more. Gunnar had known long before that day he preferred men. In an attempt to shield his reputation, he hadn't explored that side of himself as much as he would've liked. To this day, Gunnar didn't understand why he'd believed to his core Liam wouldn't say a word about anything they did, but he'd been right. Unfortunately, Liam had done such a good job pretending nothing happened, Gunnar wondered if anything had. Only the haunting dreams of Liam's moans, waking Gunnar in the middle of the night, lingered as proof. Every time, Gunnar would wake with sweat coating his body and his cock too hard to ignore. The phantom weight of Liam's lips pressed against his lingered. He could storm upstairs now and win Liam over one more time. Gunnar had already made a fool of himself by chasing the man to his work. His body didn't care Liam obviously didn't want him. The anticipation of having Liam combined with the memory of actually doing so, making Gunnar's dick throb.

Stretching out on the couch, Gunnar stared at the ceiling, wondering what Liam was doing. Was he in the shower with soap running down those sexy tattoos? Gunnar still couldn't believe how much Liam had changed. He'd obviously switched to contacts at some point in the past ten years. Gunnar approved. Liam had been sexy as hell in glasses, but the man's eyes were beyond fantastic. They deserved to shine. He'd gone from clean-cut and perfectly pressed, to sexy tousled and unkempt. Gunnar's cock twitched, reminding him of Liam's absence.

Closing his eyes, Gunnar brought a picture of Liam's sexy mouth to the forefront of his mind. It was the oddest thing. When Gunnar had chosen to stay single two years earlier, he never would've dreamed the one thing he'd miss the most would be the pressure of someone's lips against his, sharing air. Every time he kissed anyone, it only reminded Gunnar how alone he was. For some reason Gunnar couldn't explain, Liam's kiss cast a brighter light on Gunnar's loneliness than anyone else's.

The way Liam's body had moved to the music at Fusion X — damn. Gunnar could picture Liam riding his cock with the same rhythm.

Reaching down, Gunnar popped the button loose on his jeans before sliding down his zipper. He set his erection free. While fisting his cock, Gunnar recalled the sweat soaking the sheets when he'd finally gotten Liam moved from the couch to his bed. He'd left a hickey on Liam's hipbone, because he could. He'd known no one would see it. It was like it was their secret.

Liam had done things no one else had ever as much as suggested. He'd been kinky as fuck. Now, Gunnar wondered if he'd been that way because he'd always wanted to be, or if Liam was simply more sexual than most. Damn, he was willing to bet that side of Liam had only grown. A person could gain a lot of kink in ten years. A spurt of pleasure climbed up Gunnar's erection at the idea. Tightening his grip on his dick, Gunnar tugged. He needed release—relief from his fantasies and Liam.

Gunnar's balls tightened in anticipation of his orgasm. An image of Liam's full lips locked around Gunnar's dick, sucking, flared to life in Gunnar's head. Damn, he missed that heated pull. It had been too long. He didn't fuck around with just anyone, and he'd been too busy to really care. Then he'd kissed Liam. An orgasm slammed into Gunnar, taking him by surprise with its intensity. Waves of pressure transformed into pleasure as semen hit Gunnar's chest. He pumped faster, dragging out the sensation, and giving Liam his due. Not just any orgasm would do for someone like the man currently ignoring him upstairs.

When the moment passed, and the air chilled the fluid coating his torso, the bitterness set in. He'd done nothing to deserve Liam standing him up. The one night they'd spent together was years ago, and neither of them had made any promises. If they'd met a little later in life, Gunnar would've never let Liam get away. Fuck this. Gunnar shot to his feet and stormed toward the bathroom. Whipping his shirt over his head, Gunnar cleaned up his mess and found another shirt. If Liam wanted Gunnar out of his life, fine.

Heading for his computer desk, Gunnar ranted in his head with every step. Once he found what he was looking for, he calmed and questioned his judgement post orgasm. No. This was the right thing. Liam didn't want him. Gunnar always paid his debts.

# Chapter Three

A WHITE ENVELOPE held in place by a piece of tape on Liam's door stared Liam in the face as he stepped outside. He peeled it off and looked inside. A hundred-dollar bill with a Post-it note stuck to it was the only thing inside. Liam slid the money out and read the note attached.

*"Services rendered — Gunnar."*

Liam's jaw popped, making him realize how hard he'd been clenching his teeth. By going home and to bed, Liam had won the battle. Gunnar had won the war. Liam hadn't felt more like a whore in his life. As if the universe couldn't wait to find out how angry Liam truly was, Gunnar appeared from beneath the stairs. With a gym bag slung over one shoulder, Gunnar headed for his truck. Liam pulled the door closed behind him and went after him.

"What the fuck is this?" Liam asked, waving the envelope in the air at Gunnar's back. When Gunnar turned, he had one eyebrow lifted in question. Liam's mouth went dry. It wasn't fair for Gunnar to have such an effect on Liam's body, even when Liam was furious.

Gunnar unlocked his truck and threw his bag inside. "For the dance last night." Gunnar's voice said the answer should've been obvious.

"You know damn well that's not what I meant." Or maybe Gunnar didn't, but if that was the case, they couldn't ever be friends. There were some cases in life when money should never change hands. Whatever Liam and Gunnar had, it fell under those rules.

Leaning his forearms on the hood of his truck, Gunnar eyed Liam in silence for long enough that Liam had to stop himself from shifting nervously. When Liam hit the point where he couldn't take another second, he decided Gunnar wasn't worth it.

"Fuck it," Liam said, hearing the way his voice had gone dead and hating it. "I guess I know where I stand."

Liam took a step away.

"Get in the truck, Liam."

Liam froze. "Why should I?" He heard the childish tone bleeding through his question, but there it was.

Gunnar's expression never changed. "Because I told you to get in the fucking truck. Because you're obviously insulted when I was the one who got stood up. Now get in the goddamn truck."

Liam's feet moved without his permission. He couldn't deny he'd stood Gunnar up, and maybe he had earned Gunnar's wrath. It wasn't until after Liam snapped his seatbelt in place and Gunnar was backing out of his parking space that Liam thought to ask where they were headed.

"Where are we going?"

"This way," Gunnar answered, turning right.

Biting back a sigh, Liam focused on Gunnar's profile. A muscle jumped in Gunnar's jaw. It was hot. The man possessed that perfect jaw-line everyone found attractive. Since Liam had kissed it before, he found it twice as sexy. Some desires didn't need to be fed. One taste would never be enough. Gunnar glanced his way, catching Liam staring before going back to watching the road. Liam didn't stop. The vision Gunnar presented was too hot. His hair was shaved on the sides while the top was thick and soft looking. Liam wanted to run his fingers through it. Nothing good could come of the hunger gnawing at Liam's gut. The way his lips tingled with the desire to kiss Gunnar was the sort of thing that always left Liam destroyed.

"Do you mind if I ask why, if you have three unique degrees, do you still choose to do what you do? Not judging. Just curious." Gunnar's question saved Liam from spiraling out of control.

If Liam hadn't already been enraged over the money, he might've lied, but he was beyond caring what Gunnar thought of him. "I work three nights a week at Fusion X and pull in two grand a week. At first, I was paying student loans for every new idea. Then, my first niece was born, and I started spending time with her. Before too long, I had one more and realized they were my heart. So, one day, my inability to give up the money became about saving as much of it as possible."

Gunnar cast a quick glance Liam's way when it became apparent he didn't intend to say more. "Is there a connection between the money and your nieces I missed?"

"I want kids," Liam said, unashamed. Keeping his eyes locked on Gunnar, Liam watched for any reaction. He expected almost anything at this point. Gunnar merely nodded.

"Alone?"

Liam didn't hold back. "It didn't start out that way, but yes."

"How did it start?"

Liam smiled. It was out of his control. Gunnar was asking for Liam to scare him away, as far as Liam was concerned. Liam would oblige.

"With Kaz."

At his answer, Gunnar smiled, surprising him. "That explains his overprotective act at Merge last night when I stopped by to find out where you work."

"He has no right to be overprotective of me," Liam said, sounding bitter even to his ears. "He should look in the fucking mirror while remembering the way he treated me."

"Yet you're still friends," Gunnar said, pointing out the obvious.

"Yeah, well," Liam said, turning his attention to the passing scenery. "It's amazing how hard it is to go from being best friends, lovers, and living together for three years to being nothing at all. Even when you're hurt and angry," Liam added, more for himself.

Gunnar released a low whistle. "Three years, huh? What happened?"

"I happened," Liam answered, incapable of not being honest. "We were happy, doing together forever type shit. We both worked nights, so we spent our days watching TV, playing with my nieces, and going to the grocery store. You know, normal people shit. It never occurred to me that we were playing at being normal and like I said, I want it all. I want marriage, kids, the white picket fence. The whole damn thing." Liam watched the businesses come and go as they drove by. He wasn't really seeing a thing. In his head, all Liam could see was Kaz's expression when he'd realized Liam loved him for real. "When I finally found the courage to admit it, Kaz laughed. Of course, then he recognized how serious I was. Turns out, he had a different image of us than I did. He's a bouncer and I'm a stripper. That's who we are. We were together, but not seriously. You'd think I would've figured that out sooner," Liam said, hearing his hurt and not caring. He cleared his throat and shrugged. "Anyhow, we went our separate ways, but giving up on being friends turned out to be harder to let go than we expected. He kept calling and texting about the things he always had. I did the same. Anything was better than the sudden silence. Anything at all." Liam wanted to bite off his tongue as the final bit left his lips. He never stopped talking before telling too much.

Gunnar pulled into the parking lot of Trimmer's gym and circled around to the back. Liam's curiosity inched up. When Gunnar threw the truck into reverse and backed into a parking spot, Liam chuckled.

"I can't fucking believe this. This is where I work out too. How have I never seen you here?"

Instead of answering Liam's question, Gunnar asked one of his own. "Do you know what I remember most about you from high school?"

Liam shook his head since his tongue wouldn't work in the face of Gunnar's serious expression and tone.

"Your bravery," Gunnar said, sounding sincere and stealing Liam's breath. "To this day, I've never met another person as courageous as you were in the face of all adversity. If you can show a child how to be even half of what you are, you'll be an amazing dad."

Liam swallowed past the lump forming in his throat. "Thank you for that."

"Don't thank me. I'm being honest. My dad left because he wanted his freedom. You let someone go because you wanted a child. That's —" Gunnar shook his head without finishing, robbing Liam of hearing his thoughts. He wanted to beg Gunnar to finish. Instead, he motioned toward the back door of the gym.

"Why are we here?"

A bright smile lit Gunnar's face. "I promised you could watch me spar. This is where it happens."

Liam felt the tug at the corners of his mouth and gave in to his smile. "Sweet."

"Are you still mad at me?"

At Gunnar's unexpected question, Liam held the envelope out. "If you don't want me to be angry, then don't treat me like a whore."

———

SNAGGING THE MONEY FROM LIAM, Gunnar tossed it on the dashboard before closing the distance between them. "I swear, that was never my intention," Gunnar promised as he tugged Liam forward and touched his lips to Liam's. The flavor of Liam's tongue fed some addiction in Gunnar he couldn't name. All he knew was he didn't want to quit. Since they were in a public parking lot and he'd like to go inside without sporting a hard on, Gunnar pulled away, getting nowhere near enough. Liam looked every bit as turned on as Gunnar felt.

"Come on. Let's go inside before Aden comes looking for me."

After locking up Gunnar's truck, they walked side-by-side, close enough their elbows brushed, to the door.

"Who's Aden?"

The smile tugging at the corners of Gunnar's mouth was out of his control. It was part having Liam at his side, and part imagining Aden's re-action to meeting Liam. Gunnar brought no one to camp with him. "He's my trainer. I'm not sure how to prepare you for meeting him. The only thing I can say is—good luck and I'm sorry."

"Great."

Gunnar had to bite back a laugh at Liam's dry tone. He opened the door, allowing Liam to enter ahead of him. His reasons were purely selfish. Gunnar truly loved Liam's ass.

"Fuck me, Gunnar. I thought you were giving this dude's arse an Aussie kiss out there, and I'd be stuck standing round here all day." Aden switched his focus to Liam. The way his laughing green gaze transformed to wicked as it dropped to Liam's toes before slowly moving to his face made Gunnar want to throttle him. "Although I do understand the distraction. What's your name, boy?"

Anyone else would've balked at being called a boy, but Liam's good nature seemed to always win. He held his hand out for Aden to shake. "I'm Liam."

Aden looked like a giant, engulfing Liam when he shook his hand. "Eh there, Liam. You're a sexy fucker. I can't lie."

Liam winked. "Thank you. I must admit I like them big and with an accent, but I also have my eye set on Gunnar at the moment."

Gunnar had to focus on his feet to hide his re-action. First off, Aden hated everyone equally, and that didn't seem to extend to Liam. Second, Gunnar would rip Aden's spine out if he even thought about Liam again after this moment. It didn't matter Aden had three inches and seventy-five pounds on him. The big red-haired Irish fucker would go down if he thought to trespass.

Aden grunted. "He is a good-looking bastard. Suppose I'll wait my turn. Now," he said, turning his attention Gunnar's way, "you've got six days left to get ready for your next fight. Try to be on time tomorrow." As always, he turned away, headed for the ring, and dismissed Gunnar without allowing him time to make excuses. He already knew Gunnar wouldn't.

Gunnar handed his gym bag off to Liam. "Do you mind hanging on to this and saving me a trip to the locker room?"

"Since I'm the reason you're in trouble, I suppose I'd better." The heavy laughter in Liam's voice had Gunnar wanting to skip a day of training camp for the first time in years. Liam was a dangerous man. He was also a distraction. While Aden helped tape Gunnar's hands before gloving up, Gunnar split his attention between Aden's report after studying Gunnar's opponent and making a mental note of everyone who stopped to chat with Liam.

"I heard a rumor today."

Gunnar nearly groaned at Aden's random comment. He feared he knew exactly what Aden had heard. Not that he intended to say as much.

"Is that so?"

Aden kept his gaze locked on his task as he answered, confirming Gunnar's fears. "Aye. I hear he-who-shall-not-be-named, but goes who goes by 'champ' these days, mentioned you in his last press conference."

"Don't care," Gunnar said, hoping Aden would quit while he was ahead. Of course, it was Aden, so Gunnar's hopes were doomed to fail.

"You damn well should care, since he was calling you out, saying how you're the only real competitor left to beat, and if you were a real man, you'd take the challenge."

"No, thanks. Are we sparring here or you planning to talk me to death?"

Aden wouldn't be budged. "You should accept. This douche is disparaging you."

"For a man who had a lot to say about me being five minutes late, you're sure wasting a lot of time."

Without tearing his gaze away from Gunnar, Aden lifted his chin and yelled over the crowd inside the training area. "Liam."

Liam nodded at the dude talking to him before turning his attention Aden's way. "Yep."

"Tell Gunnar he should take the challenge."

That wasn't fair. Gunnar's gaze shifted to Liam at Aden's demand. Liam's eyes shone with good humor, distracting Gunnar. He looked like he was enjoying himself. The knowledge made this horrible discussion worth it.

"You should accept the challenge," Liam said without missing a beat.

Gunnar didn't feel he owed Aden shit, but Liam... Gunnar didn't know why, but he didn't want Liam to think he was backing down. "There's a lot you don't understand about this." If there was a God in Heaven, Gunnar wouldn't have to explain himself.

Liam shrugged. "I don't need to know the situation. Unless you've changed more than I ever dreamed, you're not the type to back down. If this guy keeps challenging you, and you keep refusing, he's making you look weak. I know that's not true, and I can't see you accepting such a thing."

Gunnar was floored. There'd been so many people vying for Liam's attention. He didn't think Liam had been listening to his conversation with Aden. Gunnar needed to explain.

"He's my ex," Gunnar said, getting it out in the open before this discussion went any further.

Liam shrugged again. "Even more reason for you to accept. It's one thing for a complete stranger to talk shit, but you know..."

Yeah. Gunnar knew. It wasn't as if he hadn't considered every possible scenario. Setting his forearms on the ropes, Gunnar focused on Liam. There was something about being in Liam's company. Gunnar forgot where they were. Everyone disappeared.

"In a fight, one of the most important aspects is not letting your opponent in your head. He's already in mine. I don't like accepting a bout where I'm at such a huge disadvantage from the get-go."

One corner of Liam's mouth lifted. Gunnar's chest tightened at the wicked glint in Liam's gaze. "So shove him out." Liam's expression shifted, turning thoughtful. "Unless you don't want to be the champion," he added, forcing Gunnar to search his soul.

Did he want top spot? At one time, it had been his biggest dream to be on top. Then his ex had won the title, and Gunnar had learned the hard way the man didn't love him. Everything changed. He'd settled. Was Liam right? Did he-who-shall-not-be-named get some fucked up sense of satisfaction each time he taunted Gunnar with the title, and Gunnar backed down? The idea made Gunnar want to track the bastard down and beat his cheating face in. But that was the real problem, wasn't it? The man had already humiliated Gunnar once by flaunting another lover in Gunnar's face. If Gunnar lost a bout against him, Gunnar wasn't sure how he'd handle the blow or if he'd ever try going for the top again.

"I'll think about it," Gunnar said because everyone was still looking at him, waiting for an answer.

Aden crowed in satisfaction. "That's the best news I've heard all month. 'I'll think about it' is further than I've ever gotten," he said, focusing on Liam. "Damn, Liam. You should crash training sessions more often. I can see you're the inspiration we've been lacking."

Liam winked. Gunnar wanted to punch Aden in his throat. It was obvious by the relaxed way Liam leaned against the wall, hands shoved in his pockets and enjoying the banter, he didn't realize Aden was flirting with him. Gunnar knew. Aden still had to step into the ring with Gunnar today. He didn't need to feed Gunnar's jealousy. No one was more dangerous than Gunnar when his temper ruled him.

# Chapter Four

THE DRIVE HOME was made in comfortable silence. Liam didn't seem to need anyone to entertain him or to fill the silence with useless words. Gunnar couldn't stop glancing his way, checking to see if he was still looking content. Every time Liam smiled at him sweetly, Gunnar had to stop himself from reaching over to hold Liam's hand. He could easily become attached to this man.

"I need a quick shower, but would you like to come in for some coffee?" Gunnar asked as they both slid from the truck.

Liam headed for Gunnar's front door, and a cheer rang out inside Gunnar's head. He liked Liam and wanted to spend more time with him. After the money incident, Gunnar hadn't been sure he would hear from Liam ever again once they parted ways today. Liam's willingness to stay in Gunnar's company gave him hope.

After letting Liam inside, Gunnar tossed his bag, keys, and phone onto the couch. "Give me ten minutes to clean up, and I'll start the coffee."

"Point me in the right direction, and I'll start it while you're in the shower," Liam offered.

With a dip of his chin, Gunnar waved Liam toward the kitchen. He followed on Liam's heels, blatantly watching Liam's ass with every step. It was out of his control. Liam was amazing. Gunnar pointed out where he kept everything and gave Liam a quick rundown on his overly complicated coffee maker. Once he was certain Liam would be fine without him,

Gunnar started toward his bedroom. He took two steps before making the mistake of glancing over his shoulder. Liam stood at the counter, looking like he belonged there, and sexy as sin. Before Gunnar realized he'd changed directions, Liam's hips slid across Gunnar's palms as Gunnar's arms encircled Liam's waist. He used his weight to pin Liam against the counter. With his hips cradling Liam's ass, Gunnar touched his lips to the side of Liam's neck. Liam's head dropped back onto Gunnar's shoulder in surrender.

"I swear I'll take a shower in a minute," Gunnar promised. His lips said one thing, but Gunnar's hands found their way beneath Liam's shirt. He traveled upward until reaching Liam's nipple piercings. "Seriously, I realize I'm covered in dried sweat. I just need to know something before I leave you alone." He toyed with the rings in Liam's nipples. Liam released a low moan, hardening Gunnar's dick. "Yeah. That's exactly what I've been wondering," Gunnar said, pushing away from the counter and heading for the shower before he fell on the man like a starving dog. He'd been dying to know if those rings made a difference sexually. Now that his question had been answered, Gunnar knew where he'd start next time he had Liam out of his shirt.

---

LIAM CLUNG TO THE EDGE OF THE counter like a lifeline. Gunnar had a way of leaving him wanting everything. He had no idea how long he stared at the coffeemaker in front of him, attempting to call his body under control and do as he'd planned. It wasn't happening. The sensation of Gunnar's lips on his neck, and his palms sliding up Liam's torso lingered on his skin. It had been so long since Liam allowed anyone to touch him. He hadn't wanted it. Obviously, he had needs like any man, but he had zero desire for the complications that came along with letting someone in his bed. Now, all he could think about was how Gunnar would feel, stretching him wide. Desire ruled everything inside Liam's head.

It had been sexy as fuck watching Gunnar attempt to beat the shit out of Aden. Surely he was twisted in some way for thinking so, but there it was. Liam had been at half-mast the entire time, watching Gunnar's muscles move in perfect rhythm. The thought made his stomach growl. It had nothing to do with food.

Before even he knew what he'd do, Liam's feet were moving toward Gunnar's bedroom. The door stood open. Liam stepped inside. He heard the shower curtain slide across the metal rod. Steam rolled through the open bathroom doorway. Liam's steps slowed, but he didn't stop moving. Gunnar appeared, wrapping a soft-looking dark blue towel around his hips, blocking out the light behind him. Water dripped from his hair onto Gunnar's shoulders before rolling down his chest. Liam followed the progression with his gaze. His dick throbbed in approval.

Gunnar glanced up, catching sight of Liam. Lust flared in Gunnar's eyes before his expression went blank, hiding his thoughts. "Did you need something?"

Liam bit back an evil smile at Gunnar's choice of words. "Yeah," Liam said, closing the distance between them. Snagging Gunnar's towel, he towed him forward. "You," he admitted, going up on his toes and seizing Gunnar's mouth. There'd been a hint of fear in the back of Liam's mind that Gunnar might reject him. It fled as Gunnar's hands gripped Liam's ass and lifted him from the floor. Gunnar's strength amazed Liam and heightened his lust. This man would do things to him—things from which Liam might never recover. He couldn't wait.

The room shifted and Liam found himself on his back on his Gunnar's bed, staring up at

Gunnar hovering over him. It took him a moment to realize he held Gunnar's hips between his hands—his bare hips. At some point, Gunnar had lost his towel. Liam approved. Gunnar's skin was overly warm and smelled like a man's soap. Liam wanted to lick him. When he pulled away to try it, Gunnar leaned back out of his reach and worked Liam's shirt over his head. Once he had Liam bare from the waist up, Gunnar froze.

"Are you sure about this?"

"Are you?" Liam shot back.

Gunnar smirked. "Will you pretend we didn't happen tomorrow?"

Once again, Liam didn't hesitate. "Will you?"

"Not a chance. You'll still be here."

Goddamn. This man. "Dear God, I hope you have a condom around here somewhere." Gunnar's face went blank. Liam's heart sank. "Let me guess, you don't have a condom around here."

Gunnar shook his head. "I've been single a long time. Do you have any upstairs?"

Liam groaned. "Part of me wants to argue that being single should mean you do keep condoms on hand, but since I've been single for a while now, and I don't have anything either, I guess I'd better keep my pants on."

In spite of their shit situation, Gunnar's smile grew. "We're a pair, you know. And, it's fine. What I want the most is this," Gunnar said, dipping his chin and recapturing Liam's mouth. Damn, Gunnar's tongue tasted delicious. Liam's dick ached, and—no doubt—he'd suffer from a terrible case of blue balls later. On the other hand, his heart soared. He couldn't re-member the last time he'd been this happy.

With a curl of his tongue, Gunnar licked the roof of Liam's mouth before retreating. Liam's head left the bed, chasing after him. His chest hurt at the idea of Gunnar stopping. Gunnar was right. This was amazing without the sex, and Liam wanted it.

Gunnar rolled to his side, taking Liam with him. He toyed with Liam's bottom lip. The expression he wore kept Liam hypnotized. To his soul, Liam thought no one had ever looked at him the way Gunnar did. It was as true now as it had been when they were teenagers.

"Do you remember the night I met you after work?" Gunnar's gaze never left Liam's mouth as he asked the question. All Liam could do was nod. "It was because of this," Gunnar added, tugging Liam's bottom lip down before nipping at it one more time and pulling away again. Liam could barely breathe from his lust. "I would wake up in the middle of the night, feeling like a lead weight sat on my chest while the phantom pressure of your lips lingered on mine. No one had ever kissed me before the way you did." Gunnar's gaze finally met his, and Liam's heart skipped a beat at Gunnar's intensity. "I couldn't stop craving you."

Gunnar's hand moved from Liam's mouth to his chest. Liam held his breath as Gunnar toyed with his nipple ring. He couldn't lie, getting those had hurt, but it had been totally worth it, especially with Gunnar setting Liam on fire.

"I never pictured you with something like this. It suits you." Liam wanted to thank him, but his throat was too dry. It didn't help matters that Gunnar's fingers were skimming lower, bringing chill bumps to Liam's skin. He reached the waist of Liam's jeans. His fingers dipped beneath. The air stuttered from Liam's lungs at the contact. "Nothing's changed," Gunnar admitted. "I still want to kiss you above all else, but these pants have to go. There're a million things I can do to you that don't require protection. Let's try a few," Gunnar suggested as he slowly slid down Liam's zipper. The button loosened next beneath Gunnar's touch.

Liam couldn't tear his gaze away from Gunnar's eyes.

"You're the most beautiful man I've ever seen. I've always thought so," Liam admitted before he realized it would happen. He didn't regret it. Gunnar was one of those men who made the world happy by simply existing. Gunnar set his erection free. The instant his fingers encircled Liam's cock, Liam's eyes fell closed in pleasure. He was helpless against it. Gunnar touching him was like heaven on earth.

"No one is more beautiful than you are right now," Gunnar said before covering Liam's mouth with his. Liam knew he should touch Gunnar in return in some way. He couldn't move. He was held prisoner inside his own head with Gunnar's hands on his body. "You should see the flush on your cheeks. It lights up your eyes." He boldly stroked Liam's dick. "You also chew on your bottom lip when you're turned on. I don't know if you realize you're doing it, but I can't look away."

Liam's hips rolled, meeting Gunnar's fist. Gunnar's thumb brushed Liam's slit, hitting his Prince Albert piercing. A deep moan escaped Liam. Gunnar's gaze dropped.

"Goddamn, Liam. Whatever you've been up to these past ten years, I approve."

Calling on strength he didn't know he possessed, Liam brushed Gunnar's bare hip with his fingertips. A blinding smile lit Gunnar's face as he met Liam's gaze once more. The sight blanked out Liam's mind.

"Don't take this personally, okay?"

No matter how hard he tried, Liam couldn't make Gunnar's words make sense. Gunnar obviously took Liam's silence as an agreement.

"I'm either all in or all out. Later, I'll make a run to the store, and I'll be all in. For now, I'd rather you didn't touch me or I can't be held responsible for taking you bareback. Surely, you don't want that. For now, I want to watch you come."

Liam pulled his hand away. A stupid part of his brain screamed that he didn't care, but luckily, his good sense won out. "If you're asking me to be selfish, I think I can handle it."

A low chuckle rolled from Gunnar's lips and hit Liam in the chest. He wanted that sound against his tongue.

"Would you kiss me?"

At Liam's question, Gunnar's expression went from wicked to sweet in an instant. Moving slowly, he leaned in and touched his lips to Liam's. The hand shoved between their bodies didn't relent. It was crazy how Liam could jack off every day and never match the feeling of Gunnar's palm sliding along his erection. He desperately wanted to trace the solid muscle of Gunnar's arms and chest. Gunnar was such a work of art. He deserved appreciation. Unfortunately, he didn't know how many other people had enjoyed Gunnar's perfection over the years. Liam couldn't risk the stupid part of his brain winning. Some things couldn't be taken back.

Between Gunnar's tongue and hand, Liam was on the verge of insanity. He moved mindlessly against Gunnar's touch, reaching for the oblivion Gunnar promised. The knowledge Gunnar was hard, even if he wouldn't let Liam touch him, was empowering. That was what Gunnar did for him. He made Liam feel like he could do anything. When Liam's orgasm hit, a moan came from Gunnar's throat, as if the pleasure had been his. Liam swore the sound doubled the intensity of his bliss. With his forehead pressed to Liam's, Gunnar kept his eyes squeezed closed. Liam couldn't stop staring at him. The way his nostrils flared, as if he willed his body under control, fascinated Liam in the aftermath of his destruction.

Gunnar's eyes opened. Liam's lips parted with greed. He was rocked to his core by the hunger in Gunnar's stare. His eyes seemed even lighter in coloration. Liam wanted to stare into them forever. His body hummed. His mind was blown. Liam's every emotion blared with intensity. This was what Gunnar did. He burrowed beneath the skin, leaving an imprint no one could shake.

"Don't ever stop looking at me like you are right now."

Gunnar always said the strangest things. Liam had to know.

"How am I looking at you?"

Gunnar gaze moved over Liam's face for a full minute before answering. "Like you've been blind your entire life, and I'm the first thing you've ever seen."

"In a way, that's true."

The deep grooves at the corners of Gunnar's mouth made an appearance, and his eyes shone with humor. "How so?"

"It's more of hindsight being a twenty-twenty thing. I just realized something."

"What's that?"

Post orgasmic bliss loosened Liam's tongue, making him admit what he normally wouldn't. "I should've let you keep me a secret. It would've been a million times easier seeing you on the sly than it was letting you go." And there it was. That was the real reason Liam had let Gunnar remain ignorant of who lived above him for the past two years. It had been hell acting as if they never happened. Every day had been a nightmare of knowing Gunnar lived a few houses down, and they may as well have been a thousand miles apart. As his skin cooled, and Gunnar's silence stretched on, Liam wished he'd kept his mouth shut. "It was a long time ago," Liam added, because his pride needed the last word.

Gunnar's expression had turned serious at Liam's confession. It didn't change. He shook his head. "Thanks for that."

Liam tried smiling without luck. "For what?"

"Telling me," Gunnar answered. "For a long time, I thought I must be ridiculously easy to forget, because you seemed to do so like it was nothing."

"Definitely not."

Gunnar's smile returned. He snagged the sheet, cleaning off Liam's chest before tossing it aside, and settling back down. He opened his arms, giving Liam a delicious view of Gunnar's body. "Can I hold you for a little while?"

How two people could be so different yet equally pathetic was beyond Liam, but he was thankful for it. "Try to kick me out and see what happens," he said, settling down in Gunnar's hold with his head on Gunnar's chest and his leg thrown over Gunnar's. "I can be damnably octopus-like when I want," To prove his point, he tightened his hold on Gunnar's body, as if wrapping himself around him. No doubt, Gunnar could easily break his hold, but as Liam hoped, Gunnar laughed instead.

"Damn. You're right. I guess I'm stuck."

Liam's cheeks hurt from smiling too much. He couldn't stop. Even as Gunnar's breathing deepened, and the man dozed off, the corners of Liam's mouth continued pulling into a grin—no matter how hard he fought to control it. There was no better way to spend a day.

WARM LIPS LANDED IN THE CENTER OF HIS spine, pulling Gunnar from sleep. They moved lower. Gunnar stretched and leaned into the touch. His balls grew heavier by the second. As his eyes opened, a smile pulled at his lips at the sight greeting him. A box of condoms and a bottle of lube sat near his head. Gunnar rolled, leaving Liam no other choice but to climb aboard or end up squashed.

The soft skin of Liam's inner thighs brushed Gunnar's hips, making his eyes fall closed for a moment. He missed the weight of someone straddling his body. Liam's lips touched the center of Gunnar's chest, pulling his eyes open again. He brushed his fingers through Liam's hair.

"I didn't hear you leave."

Glancing up the line of Gunnar's body, Liam set his chin on Gunnar's chest as he responded. "I didn't. There's this app on my phone where I can get anything available in this area delivered for a fee. It was worth the fee."

Gunnar's stomach shook in his silent laughter. "Smart thinking." Gunnar's praise died on a moan as Liam slid lower, opening his mouth over Gunnar's hipbone, and palming Gunnar's erection. He rocked into Liam's touch, incapable of holding still. By the time Liam's lips closed around the head of Gunnar's cock, a fine sheen of sweat already coated Gunnar's skin. His stomach quivered at the first light lick and gentle suction. Liam took him an inch deeper. Gunnar gripped the sheets beside him and held on. The soft brush of Liam's tongue had Gunnar gritting his teeth. In his head, Gunnar held Liam's hair in a vise-like grip and fucked the man's mouth as hard as Liam could stand it. In truth, he didn't want Liam's torture to ever stop. His feather-light ministrations combined with impressive deep throating had Gunnar a mess. Gunnar wanted to fuck Liam with something akin to desperation, but he also didn't want Liam to stop. Not for the first time in his life, he kind of wished he had two dicks. Liam pulled away and sat back on his heels. The pained groan leaving Gunnar's lips was out of his control.

"I want to be inside you too badly to hate you, but it's a near thing."

Liam chuckled at Gunnar's discomfort. It sounded evil as hell. "Don't worry. I'll take care of you, but I want you inside me when you come."

The vision of Liam sitting on Gunnar's thighs, dick hard and glistening with pre-cum as he rolled a condom down Gunnar's length before slathering it with lube, was by far the hottest thing Gunnar had ever seen. That was saying something because he'd seen a lot. Liam crawled up Gunnar's body, positioning himself over Gunnar's cock. Every muscle in Gunnar's body tensed with anticipation. He knew Liam was doing all the work, but Gunnar couldn't move. Liam owned him in that moment. With Gunnar's erection held tight, Liam lowered himself onto Gunnar's dick. A sharp pain radiated though Gunnar's lip, making him realize he'd been biting it—expectant.

The tight heat squeezing his cock competed with Liam's expression for biggest turn on. Gunnar wondered which would cripple him first. "I won't last long," Gunnar admitted.

"You're too fucking amazing and I've been celibate too long."

Liam froze, holding Gunnar's gaze. "How long is too long?"

"Almost two years," Gunnar confessed without an ounce of shame.

A smile exploded across Liam's face as he lowered his head. An inch away from Gunnar's lips, Liam paused. "I promise I'll be gentle." With Liam's vow hanging between them, Liam opened his mouth over Gunnar's. If there was any mercy in the world, Liam wouldn't hold true to his word. Gunnar needed Liam's destruction. The walls that kept him to himself the past two years had begun crumbling the moment he'd recognized Liam. Liam was exactly the man he'd been waiting for. Someone he already trusted. Someone who'd been a dormant desire, lingering inside of him.

The fantasies Liam created the night before as he'd danced in Gunnar's lap, he brought to life now. The strength, talent, and amazing balance he'd shown hovering over Gunnar's chair were happening on Gunnar's dick, and Gunnar couldn't breathe. He kept losing touch with reality, forgetting his place, until he was certain Liam did all the work. All Gunnar did was feel. Every sensation and tug of his cock increased the pressure crawling up his erection. It hit a point when Gunnar feared for Liam's safety. Liam's cum coated the space between their bodies, making things worse. Somehow, he'd pleased Liam, but damned if he knew how at this point.

Liam's moans filled Gunnar's ears and his bottom lip stung from Liam's biting kisses. All Gunnar could focus on was the spring winding tighter inside him. When it finally snapped, a gasp tore from Gunnar's throat, pulling Liam's name out along with all the oxygen from Gunnar's body. His arms locked around Liam's body, crushing him against his chest, but Gunnar couldn't stop. The massive waves causing his dick to dance inside Liam's ass rendered him helpless. Liam seized Gunnar's mouth in an almost violent kiss. If they needed oxygen to survive, neither one showed it. Liam was the first to pull away. Luckily, he didn't go far. He buried his face in the crook of Gunnar's neck. His ragged breathing almost matched the pounding of Gunnar's pulse beating in his ears.

"Oh my God."

Gunnar nodded in wholehearted agreement with Liam's sentiment.

"What just happened?"

Gunnar shook his head at Liam's question. "I'm not sure, but I think we may have found our way back to where we should've been all along, and I'm also wondering if my bed survived the earthquake." Every word came out on a gasp as Gunnar fought to breathe. The way Liam's body shook with laughter made any brain damage Gunnar suffered worthwhile.

GUNNAR LEFT LIAM HALF ASLEEP WHILE he went for a run. Restless energy kept him moving when he really wanted to get back to Liam. With his upcoming fight looming on the horizon, Gunnar couldn't shirk his training duties, no matter the bad timing. The concrete smacking the bottom of his shoes was the only thing that felt the least bit realistic in the aftermath of Liam. It was funny how his anger had kept him from noticing the two years he'd spent not touching anyone else. With his lips still tingling from Liam's stinging kisses, Gunnar didn't think he could go back to that solitary lifestyle. That was bad.

Caring about someone else had destroyed Gunnar. It always demolished Gunnar. For years, he'd trained while having the occasional fling. His mother had gotten sick, and life had become a balancing act. He'd somehow kept his win ratio high while caring for her. She was the only person he'd ever loved, and he'd been slowly losing her. Maybe that was why he'd been so easy to deceive when he'd met his ex. Perhaps that grief had kept him blind. Not that it mattered, he'd ended up losing everything at the same time. His mom. The man he loved. His dreams of becoming champion.

By the time Gunnar made it back home, an odd darkness loomed over his thoughts, threatening to pull him under. The moment he stepped inside his bedroom and heard the shower running, it disappeared, as if Liam possessed some magic. He stripped as he headed for the shower, dropping his clothes as he went. Liam's chin rested on his chest as the man let the hot water stream over him. Without giving Liam a chance to stop him, Gunnar stepped inside the shower with him, engulfing him in his embrace.

Liam relaxed into his hold. The backs of Gunnar's eyes burned unexpectedly. People used him—always had. They wanted him for reasons all their own, but never because they craved his company. There was something about Liam. He felt different from everyone else. Was it possible he was slipping back into some vulnerable place in his life where he'd easily allow some man to destroy him again? He didn't know. His bouts of severe depression always came with no warning. Most times, he didn't realize they'd set in until it was too late.

"This is how people should shower every day," Liam said, sounding content.

Gunnar pressed his lips to Liam's shoulder. "Agreed." Especially since it didn't feel sexual. It felt intimate. Liam turned in his arms. His expression was sweet, captivating Gunnar.

"You make me feel lazy with all this sparring and running."

Gunnar shook his head. "It's only because I have a fight coming up. I don't like you feeling bad because of me. You're perfect."

An odd look passed over Liam's features. Whatever floated through the other man's head, he kept it to himself. Instead, he reached around Gunnar and grabbed the body wash. "Here," Liam said, squeezing some into his hand. "Let me take care of you."

Gunnar stood still as Liam washed him. His gaze ate up every detail and sensation. Liam did a damn good job of making Gunnar feel pampered. By the time he finished scrubbing every inch of Gunnar's body, the water ran cold, and Gunnar was grateful for it. He needed cooling off. They needed to eat. If they kept this up, Gunnar would be inside Liam in moments, and he wanted Liam to feel as important as Liam made him feel.

With nothing except towels wrapped around their waists, they made their way toward the kitchen, taking turns stealing touches. Gunnar pulled out a stool at the bar and motioned for Liam to take a seat. Liam accepted. After grabbing Liam a bottle of water, Gunnar found some fruit in the fridge and set to slicing it. For some strange reason, as Gunnar made Liam a plate, he thought of his friend, Troy. They'd met almost two months earlier when Gunnar had been in New Orleans for a fight. Troy had looked sad, and Gunnar had wanted to fix it. Of course, there had been a million things he hadn't realized about Troy at the time. One slow dance, two hours of conversation, and a stolen kiss hadn't lifted Troy's spirits. But they'd both walked away with a new friend.

His next fight was in Troy's hometown of Phoenix. He should go see him while he was there. Damn. Gunnar didn't want to leave Liam yet. "I have this friend in Phoenix who was in a horrible car accident about a month ago. It fucked him up pretty good. He lost a leg and his sister died." Gunnar wasn't sure why he was telling Liam this. Since Troy's accident, Gunnar had been going through the motions with no one to talk to about it. It was a fucked up thing, being completely alone in the world.

"That's awful," Liam said, sounding as if he meant it.

It was. Gunnar hated what Troy was going through. "Yeah," he agreed absently. "I feel horrible for him. Work takes me out that way quite a bit, and I've been by the hospital a few times to see him, but he's always out of it when I go by there." A low chuckle escaped Gunnar. "Plus, he's got this huge ass hockey player wrapped around his finger, and that dude's been guarding the door like an avenging angel, refusing to let anyone disturb Troy." Gunnar kind of wanted to kick himself once the words were out there. "Don't repeat that, okay? I gather they're keeping their relationship a secret for some reason or another, even though it's ridiculously obvious to everyone they're in love."

Liam snorted. "Who would I tell?" Liam's claim brought Gunnar's gaze his way. There were moments when Liam reminded Gunnar so much of himself. Did he not have anyone to talk to either? "Besides," Liam added. "You have nothing to worry about with me. Even if I knew these people, I'd never say anything. Living openly isn't equally easy for everyone. Sometimes there's other shit to consider."

It was just another example of why Liam was so amazing. He'd always been empathetic of others, even at the expense of himself. Gunnar moved to where Liam sat. After setting a plate in front of him, Gunnar squeezed Liam's shoulders, hugging the man to his chest.

"I trust you," Gunnar said, surprising himself with how much he meant it. "But I brought it up for a reason," Gunnar admitted, realizing now why Troy had popped into his head. "I'm headed that way in a few days for a fight. If you can, I'd love for you to go with me."

Liam's shoulders shook with laughter. "Care to narrow that timeline down?"

"Leave Thursday. Come back Sunday," Gunnar answered immediately, recognizing his mistake. His heart sank. Liam worked weekends. The odds of him going with Gunnar would be slim.

"Sure. I can do that."

"Really?" Gunnar heard the hope in his voice and was incapable of squashing it. "I worried you wouldn't be able to miss work."

Tilting his chin up, Liam met Gunnar's stare. "Obviously, I can't take off every weekend, since that's when the most money rolls in, but I don't have a set schedule. I can do whatever."

Gunnar pressed his lips to Liam's temple. He tried stamping down his growing happiness without much luck. It was hard with Liam bringing so much light to his day. "Are you sure? I want you with me, but not if it's costing you too much."

Liam chuckled, making Gunnar want to feel the sound against his skin. "I can handle one weekend away, especially if it makes you smile like you're doing now. I like that shit."

"Do you now?" Gunnar asked, ready to play. He skimmed his fingers down Liam's ribs. "What else do you like?"

"To eat," Liam said, as if admitting a dirty secret and bringing a strawberry slice to his lips. "Seriously," he added as he chewed. "I'm starving."

With a forlorn sigh, Gunnar moved to fix his plate. "I guess I can let you do that."

The chuckle following in the wake of his claim made it worthwhile. Maybe Gunnar would get hurt if he kept seeing Liam. Maybe he wouldn't. Either way, Gunnar couldn't stop wanting Liam at his side. Their trip to Phoenix couldn't get there fast enough to suit him.

## Chapter Five

GUNNAR HATED HOSPITALS. He'd spent way too much time visiting them during his mom's final months. The smell. The hopelessness hanging in the air. He fucking despised the place, but something drove him to see Troy. The night they'd met, Troy had seemed broken in a way Gunnar understood too well. Now, the man had lost a leg and a sister. Life was an evil bitch. When Troy's room came into view, Gunnar pasted on his biggest smile, determined to bring happiness to a bleak situation.

"Jesus Christ," Gunnar cried as he sailed inside Troy's hospital room, catching sight of a gigantic plant sitting in the corner and sticking out as the world's worst eyesore. "Who sent the huge-ass plant?"

"Hey," Troy called, sounding genuinely happy to see him. "I didn't know you were in town."

Gunnar shrugged as he pulled a chair closer to Troy's bed. It seemed he always changed planes in Phoenix on his way to someplace else, but in this case, he had all weekend, and he needed to know Troy was okay. He'd forgotten how sexy the other man's green eyes were. Liam filled his head now. "You know me. I'm always blowing through town when I can. I came as soon as I heard about your accident, but you're not likely to remember it. Now, seriously, who sent the tree?"

Troy spared the expensive foliage a quick glance before averting his eyes from it. Gunnar was certain Troy hoped Gunnar wouldn't notice, but he did. "Mara King."

Troy's answer was the last one Gunnar had been expecting. "The actress?"

Animosity coated Troy's every word. "The one and only."

There was a story there, Gunnar was sure of it. Mara King was one of the biggest actresses in Hollywood, and she'd sent Troy a tree. Gunnar released a low whistle. "Wow. That's really..." He struggled for a way to describe the plant. "...one monstrously large bush."

Troy didn't laugh as Gunnar hoped. "It's probably proportionate to her guilt," Troy grumbled under his breath.

Yep. Definitely a story there. Gunnar eyed him curiously while Troy tried to avoid his stare. He searched his mind for any gossip he'd ever heard about Mara King. Her popularity as an actress couldn't be matched, but otherwise...the memory slid in, and Gunnar knew exactly why Troy obviously hated her. He opened the conversation, wondering if Troy would admit it.

"You know, I think I remember hearing a rumor about her dating Noah at one time." Noah was Troy's gigantic hockey player—the secret.

Troy's eyes skirted away. "I'm getting sprung tomorrow," Troy said, changing the subject and making Gunnar want to growl. Troy was openly gay. Noah was not. It was a sad situation for both of them as long as they kept this up. Anyone who bothered to look could see they were in love. There was only one reason Gunnar could think of for them to keep their relationship secret—Noah's reputation. Unfortunately, only one of them really got hurt in that equation.

Gunnar tried allowing Troy to change the subject. "Then it's a good thing I stopped by today. I've been by a couple of times, but you were always out of it, and Noah was hovering over you like Papa Bear." Nope. He couldn't let it go. No good could come of these two keeping their relationship hidden. First off, it was obviously destroying them. Secondly, Troy deserved better. Thirdly, Gunnar fucking hated secrets. They destroyed good people.

Troy's teeth went for his bottom lip. He visibly fought back a smile at the mention of Noah's name. "Yeah. I guess he's been a bit..."

Gunnar couldn't take anymore. "Dude loves you for real," Gunnar said, pointing out the obvious.

Troy kept his eyes locked on the opposite wall, still trying to hide his feelings. It drove Gunnar batshit. "We've been best friends since Pre-K," Troy said, filling the air with a half-truth. "If roles were reversed, I'd be the same."

Gunnar snorted. "You'd be the same because you love him too."

Finally, Troy met his gaze, making Gunnar understand the full force of why he hadn't done so before now. Everything Troy felt was on display. His anger. His love. Everything. That's what love did. It consumed everyone involved, destroying them from the inside out. One of two things came of such strong emotions—a bond forged of steel or two individuals left damaged beyond all repair.

Gunnar shook his head. "The two of you love each other all the way," Gunnar said, tired of being lied to and needing to speak his piece. "This isn't friendship. Don't get me wrong, you being best friends is an awesome foundation for what the two of you have going on, but I'm not blind, and neither is anyone else."

No response came.

Gunnar smiled, trying to lighten the mood. After all, Troy had been through enough. "It might surprise you to know I haven't always been so don't-give-a-fuck-about-society as I am now. I used to be just like your boy Noah."

Troy held his silence, but didn't look away.

Gunnar took it as permission to go on. "Back when I first hit the professional boxing scene, my reputation meant everything to me. Hell, it was all I had. All I wanted was to be the best. I'd known my whole life I preferred men, but I kept that part of myself separate from my career." Unfortunately, opening this topic had the adverse effect of reminding Gunnar he'd done the same shit to Liam years ago that Noah was now doing to Troy. He turned inside himself, absorbing the memories of all he'd been through to get to this point. "It wasn't hard. I spent so much time training, I didn't have any free time for play anyhow. For the most part, I just shut the door on that side of myself while I focused on winning the next bout." A small smile touched Gunnar's lips. "Then, one day, everything changed."

"What happened?" Troy asked, sounding fascinated.

Gunnar focused on Troy almost having forgotten his presence. He hated thinking of his ex —loathed every breath the man took. When Gunnar responded, his voice came out sounding dead, even to his ears. He couldn't stop it from happening. Gunnar regretted having taken this path to help Troy.

"I met a force of nature who refused to stay on the sidelines." Even saying the words tasted like ash. "You know, when someone touches you in just the right way, and your eyes fall closed? All you know is bliss, and no one else will do. You'd go to any length to feed the addiction." A wry smile twisted Gunnar's lips. "Every time he touched me, it was like that. It messed me up, man," Gunnar said with a shake of his head. Gunnar cleared his throat. "Anyhow, I'm sorry about your sister," Gunnar said, ruthlessly changing the subject and hating himself for it. "That's a tough road, and there's nothing I can say to fix it, but I'm around if you need me. You still have my number?"

Troy looked around as if he'd forgotten where they were. "Um, I'm not sure."

Gunnar pulled his phone out and found Troy's number. He sent him a quick text, ensuring his number would show up on Troy's device. "There. I've sent you a text. Make sure you save me in your contacts."

As Troy opened his mouth, a buzzing noise cut through the silence and obviously distracted the man from whatever he'd planned to say. He focused on the table across the room where a phone sat. Gunnar moved to snag it and handed it over.

"Save my number while you're still thinking about it."

Troy swiped his finger across the face of the phone's screen. "I guess I do still have it, since your name is already showing." He flashed the phone Gunnar's way, showing the proof.

Gunnar spared a glance for the device in Troy's hand. "Cool. Make sure you use it if you need anything."

"I will," Troy promised.

Gunnar stood. "I'm gonna head out before Noah shows up and throws me out." An uncomfortable laugh accompanied his words. He wished now he'd never tried interfering with Troy's relationship. It wasn't as if he was in some secure place in life where he knew better than others.

Troy looked thoughtful for a moment before responding. "Thanks for coming to see me. It means a lot."

"Of course," Gunnar shot back immediately. "That's what friends do." With a wink, Gunnar headed for the door.

Before he could make his getaway, Troy called out, stopping him. "Hey, what happened to the guy you were telling me about?"

Gunnar kept his gaze locked on the doorframe. He'd been so close to never having to talk about this again. "His eyes didn't fall closed when I touched him back." As the words left his lips, realization struck—Liam's did. Every single time Gunnar touched him. Well, hell. He needed to get back and make it happen again. Only an idiot would pass on what Gunnar had waiting for him back at the room.

———

THE HOTEL ROOM GUNNAR HAD BOOKED for them was nicer than Liam expected. It wasn't that he thought Gunnar was cheap or anything. It was more that the place seemed excessive for a weekend away. When Liam had tried explaining as much to Gunnar, Gunnar had laughed and confessed the casino had provided the room as part of his contract for the fight. With that mystery solved, Liam chose to enjoy the place as much as possible while Gunnar went to visit his friend in the hospital. Liam didn't feel right, showing up during a stranger's time of need and imposing, so he'd stayed behind. The hotel's bottom floor had the shining lights of over three thousand slot machines and hundreds of gaming tables. He felt confident in his ability to lose a ton of money while Gunnar was away.

At a hundred dollars down, Liam figured out a strategy that kept him from losing any more money while allowing him another hour of entertainment. He could feel the eyes of two old ladies boring into his back, waiting for the moment he left his machine. His phone buzzed in his back pocket. Since the casino didn't allow any electronic devices on the floor, Liam cashed out and headed for the elevator before checking his messages.

Gunnar: *What are you doing right now?*

Liam stepped onto the elevator before responding.

Liam: *Leaving the casino and heading for the room.*

Gunnar: *Win any money?*

Liam: *Ha!*

Gunnar: *I'd hoped to catch you nude or something.*

Liam: *You're not here to enjoy it.*

The doors slid open on the top floor, and Liam stepped out. He kept one eye on making sure he didn't walk into anything while checking his phone with the other.

Gunnar: *How do you know? You're not in the room.*

Liam: *Obviously you aren't either if you're asking about being nude.*

The smile Liam wore was out of his control.

Gunnar: *I didn't ask. I pointed out I'd hoped to catch you nude.*

The room came into view as well as the "do not disturb" sign. Liam slid his phone back in his pocket and dug out his room card. When the door swung wide, Liam was met with darkness. A spurt of disappointment ran through him. Pushing the door closed behind him, Liam felt along the wall, trying to find the light switch. Before he had time to find it, a solid weight slammed into his back, catching him off guard. Gunnar's familiar scent surrounded him before Liam found himself crowded against the wall.

"I've been waiting," Gunnar said before nipping at the side of Liam's neck.

Liam pressed his forehead to the wall, sucking in a deep breath and attempting to call his racing heart under control. He could feel Gunnar's erection against his ass. Liam's dick hardened in response.

"Hopefully, not for long." Even Liam heard the breathless note to his voice.

"Only about ten minutes," Gunnar admitted, running his tongue down the cords of Liam's neck until he reached where they met his shoulder. He placed a light kiss there as his hands found their way beneath Liam's shirt. "It was about eleven minutes too long. I was ready to come searching for you."

Liam's jeans loosened around his waist. "Jesus," he breathed, wondering if he'd survive Gunnar's intensity.

"Damn. I want to fuck you. It's all I've thought about for the past hour."

Liam's mouth went dry. He was panting and Gunnar hadn't done much other than talk. Cool air touched his hip as Gunnar tugged one side of Liam's jeans down. "The idea of having you riding my dick made it damn near impossible to get from the car to the room without embarrassing myself." The other side of Liam's jeans moved lower. "First, I need a taste of this gorgeous ass." Gunnar fell to his knees, taking Liam's jeans and underwear with him. Liam moaned into the wood, supporting his head, as Gunnar's teeth sank into the flesh of his ass cheek. At Gunnar's urging, Liam stepped free of his pants. The instant they were gone, Gunnar tugged Liam's hips back and went all in.

With his palms flattened against the wall, Liam held on as Gunnar ate at his ass and tugged at his erection. He choked on a whimper as Gunnar shot back to his feet.

"I'm sorry, baby. I can't wait."

Liam didn't need Gunnar's apology. He didn't want to wait.

Gunnar probed Liam's asshole with his erection while licking at Liam's ear. "Don't worry, I'm already suited up and ready for you."

"Don't care," Liam panted out between breaths. "Just fuck me."

With a surge of his hips, Gunnar impaled Liam on his cock. His fingers dug into Liam's hips, holding him in place while he controlled their motions. Liam had never felt so full or manhandled. He loved it.

"Goddamn, Liam. You're so hot and tight on my dick. I wish you knew how good you make me feel." Gunnar pivoted his hips as he made the claim, going deeper, and hitting something Liam loved. The sound of their skin slapping and Gunnar's heated words were the only sounds penetrating Liam's lust.

Gunnar bit Liam's lobe as he jacked Liam's dick. He increased his speed, making Liam's head spin. "This is what I do to myself in the shower every time I think of you."

An image of Gunnar, head thrown back, cords straining in his neck, and teeth bared as he stroked his dick, flared to life in Liam's mind at

Gunnar's claim. A blinding orgasm ripped through Liam, making lights pop behind his closed lids. Rambled words left his lips, but even Liam didn't know what they were. All he knew was how his body felt beneath Gunnar's touch.

Gunnar's teeth sank into Liam's shoulder. "Oh my God, Liam. Fuck. Yeah." He felt Gunnar's body tense before a gasp tore from his throat. "Damn," Gunnar said, panting against Liam's skin. "You make me weak-kneed while simultaneously making me believe I can take over the world."

Before Liam had time to process Gunnar's claim, Gunnar snagged the hem of Liam's shirt and eased it over his head, keeping him from the mess coating the material. Once Liam was stripped bare, Gunnar swept Liam into his arms and headed for the bed.

"I'm going to be so fucking tired tomorrow for my fight, but I don't care."

Guilt overwhelmed Liam. "Oh, no. I didn't even think of that. I don't want to put you at a disadvantage."

"You could never do that," Gunnar said, tossing Liam on the bed and covering his body with his own. "Plus, it's on me. I can't keep my hands off you. Every time I touch you, your eyes fall closed, and a flush rushes to your cheeks. It's so fucking hot."

Liam kissed the column of Gunnar's neck. "I can't help it. Every time you touch me, I feel it in my chest."

Leaning away slightly, Gunnar slid his fingers along Liam's jaw before forcing his chin up. Even in the dark, he could make out the way Gunnar's eyes glittered. "That's because you care about me," Gunnar said, making Liam's throat tighten. Liam couldn't deny it.

"I do."

"Good," Gunnar said, leaning down and touching his lips to Liam's. "I care about you too. It also occurs to me I should've told you before now that we're exclusive."

Pure joy flooded Liam's veins. "Agreed." They should've had this conversation before now, and under different circumstances, but Liam didn't give a shit how the conversation came about. Gunnar had said he wanted them to be exclusive. Liam might never come down from the high of finally having Gunnar after all this time.

⸻

Sweat glistened on Gunnar's chest and arms. The shorts he wore were the same odd shade of bluish-green as his eyes. He bounced on his toes and shifted from foot to foot. Intensity bled from his every pore as he kept his gaze locked on his opponent. Liam had never been to a boxing match before. It was loud. Every punch thrown Gunnar's way made Liam want to beat the shit out of someone. By the third round, he wasn't so sure he could stand witnessing too many of Gunnar's bouts. Liam wasn't sideline material. He was hit-him-again-and-see-what-happens-motherfucker material.

Every blow seemed ridiculously ear splitting, considering the sheer volume of the crowd. Gunnar's opponent could've been anyone on the planet for all the attention Liam paid him. He was brown. That was about all Liam knew. He had brown hair, light brown skin that looked like spray tan to Liam, and—no doubt—brown eyes. The only splash of color on the scene was his red shorts.

Even without knowing much about the sport, Liam knew the guy was doing a shit job of protecting his face. It seemed every jab that landed hit the man dead on. He went down on one knee. Gunnar jumped back out of the ref's way and bounced from side to side, waiting. Liam held his breath. Gunnar's opponent pushed back to his feet but stayed bent at the waist. The count continued.

A bell sounded, and the crowd erupted, threatening to burst Liam's eardrums. The announcement came. "Hanging on to his title as the Casino champ..." Liam didn't hear the rest. His focus was all about Gunnar. Gunnar sought him out with his gaze. Someone raised one of Gunnar's arms. Instead of raising the other, as he'd always seen people do, Gunnar touched his glove to his mouth before pointing Liam's way. Lights flashed in Liam's face. He ignored them. The pride building in his chest and the smile stretching his lips were out of Liam's control. A short burst of laughter escaped Liam as a random thought snuck in. This was so much better than any of the local hot spots Gunnar could've taken him to all those years ago.

"You haven't said what you thought of the match." Gunnar hated asking, but Liam had been damnably tight lipped. He didn't need praise, but yeah, he kind of did. Gunnar was tired of switching his attention between the clouds passing by outside the plane's window and wondering over Liam's thoughts.

Liam tore his gaze away from the in-flight magazine he'd been staring at for the past ten minutes. "You were a scary level of sexy in that ring. Look at this shirt," Liam said, shaking the magazine at him. "It's perfect for you."

With an inner sigh, Gunnar leaned over and inspected the page Liam pointed out. There weren't any shirts.

Liam's lips touched Gunnar's ear. "Ha." He chuckled, bringing chill bumps to Gunnar's skin. "I have you now." He placed a light kiss against the shell of Gunnar's ear. "You were amazing, but that's no different from any other day of the week. If you need reassuring, wait until we're back home. I'll get on my knees and worship you the way you deserve." Liam's lips brushed Gunnar's skin once more. Between Liam's words and light kisses, Gunnar's mouth was dry and his dick was hard.

Lifting his arm, Gunnar urged Liam to lean into his side. "Share that magazine. I'm bored." With a smile, Liam shifted closer until there wasn't an inch between them. Once Gunnar had Liam where he wanted him, Gunnar pressed his lips to Liam's temple and spoke against his skin. "You're the one who's amazing. What do you have planned for tomorrow?"

Liam turned the page as he answered, "My sister is bringing the girls by to stay with me while she works."

Even though Gunnar knew he had to share Liam occasionally, he still didn't want to give up a minute of Liam's time. No way would he be an ass and say as much since he knew how much Liam loved his nieces.

"That's awesome. You should have fun."

"I should," Liam agreed, somehow managing to snuggle closer. "Until then, I intend to enjoy myself right here."

A hint of devilry overcame Gunnar. He touched his lips to the shell of Liam's ear, keeping his words for Liam alone. "You'll enjoy it; of that, you can be sure. I haven't fully explored this Prince Albert yet. The only way I'll ever understand your reasoning behind it is if I lick it while you describe every sensation." A flush hit Liam's cheeks and Gunnar knew Liam was hard for him. He loved tormenting Liam. Gunnar could keep that shit up all night. That wasn't the only thing Gunnar could keep up all night. "As a matter of fact," Gunnar added, "I think I should kick back and relax while you fuck my throat as long as you'd like. I promise it would be willing and eager."

"This is going to be a long flight." The breathless note to Liam's voice pulled an evil chuckle from Gunnar.

"Yeah, it is, but when we get home, I'll make it worth every torturous second," Gunnar promised. If Gunnar never kept another vow, he would make good on this. Liam would never think the same way about flying after today.

***

"Judging by the smile you're wearing, I'm going out on a limb and say you've met someone new."

Liam's cheeks ached as his grin grew. He couldn't deny his sister's observation. He hadn't stopped smiling since meeting Gunnar. It had been doubly bad after the weekend they'd spent together. He couldn't keep the news to himself a second longer. "Not someone new, per se."

Bree jumped in place, making her blond curls bounce. "Oh my God. You've gotten back together with Kaz, haven't you?"

"Nope," Liam said, drawing out the word and torturing Bree. It was one of his favorite pastimes.

Bree's face screwed up in thought. Her dark blue eyes narrowed at him. "Then, what the fuck? How's it not something new? You've never been serious with anyone else important."

He couldn't contain it a second longer. "I'm dating Gunnar Hutchinson. Well, it used to be Hutchinson. Now it's Samson. Turns out, he had it changed near the end of his senior year, but I never heard anything. Of course, as you know, I made a point of never hearing anything Gunnar-related, on account of... well, you know." She really should, since Bree was the only person on the planet, other than Gunnar, who knew about their fling all those years ago.

"Oh my God. You're rambling. You never ramble. The only time I've ever heard you ramble was when you'd decided to ask Kaz to marry you. Holy fuck! I can't believe you're dating Gunnar, and it's serious, because otherwise, you wouldn't be rambling."

"Holy fuck," Willa said, doing a damn good job of sounding exactly like her mother.

Liam chuckled.

Bree barely spared her youngest a glance. "Hush, Willa. You know you're not supposed to repeat Momma's bad words. Oh my God," Bree said again, looking almost as excited as Liam felt. "I heard he's twice as hot as he was back then, and that has to be pretty goddamn hot." She looked thoughtful for a second. "You know, I could almost hate you. You've had more action from sexy ass than any girl I know. In my next life, I'm coming back as a gay man."

Liam shook his head. "That's so fucking stupid, Bree. You're a woman. You get to sleep with men now."

"Not Gunnar," she shot back.

"Well, you're married."

"And he's gay," Bree finished, as if her point had been made. She bounced on her toes, looking exactly like the younger sister he'd grown up with rather than the—somewhat—responsible female she'd grown into. "Holy fuck. You're dating Gunnar."

"Holy fuck."

Bree sighed. "For fuck's sake, Willa. Stop saying fuck."

Liam snorted. "Your kids are hopeless. I don't know why you try."

One of Bree's shoulders lifted in a careless shrug. "Dakota starts school next year. I keep hoping if I fuss enough, I won't end up looking like the douchiest mother on the planet."

A knock landed on the door. Liam moved to answer. "Good luck with that." He swung the door wide, and happiness stood on the other side, smiling as if the feeling was mutual. "Hey, baby. I didn't think I'd see you today."

Gunnar stepped inside and planted a quick kiss at the corner of Liam's mouth. "You know I can't pass up finally meeting these kids you adore."

"Holy fuck."

At the girlish exclamation, Gunnar glanced past Liam, and a bark of laughter escaped him. Liam bit back a chuckle and turned as well. Bree gave Willa a small pat on the head.

"Holy fuck, indeed," Bree muttered before stepping forward with her hand outstretched. "Gunnar. Wow. It's only been forever."

As Gunnar shook hands with Bree, Liam mouthed "mine" behind his back. Yes, it was childish, but he didn't care. It was Bree. She already knew he was an idiot.

"I know it makes me a terrible person, but I don't remember you," Gunnar confessed, and Liam mouthed "ha" while he still had the chance. "In my defense," Gunnar added, "I get hit in the head a lot."

Willa tugged at the hem of Bree's shirt. She lifted her daughter into her arms without ever taking her gaze from Gunnar. "I'm not surprised. About you not remembering me, that is. I was a freshman when you graduated. Plus, I'm guessing you weren't checking out the incoming girls." Bree punctuated her statement with a horrified-sounding snort, and Liam grabbed his stomach, wondering if he'd rupture something laughing. "This is my youngest, Willa," Bree said, quickly changing the subject. She pointed to where Liam's oldest niece sat at the bar, coloring. "And that's my oldest, Dakota."

"They're both adorable."

Willa preened under Gunnar's praise while Dakota didn't bother glancing up.

"Of course they are," Bree agreed, handing Willa off to Liam and pressing a loud kiss to the little girl's cheek. "They both look like their dad." Moving to Dakota's side, Bree bent to hug her.

"Mommy thinks she'll never have sex unless she comes back as a gay man," Dakota informed Gunnar without looking his way.

Bree kissed Dakota on top of her head. "No. Mommy thinks she'll never have sex because neither of you girls think you have to sleep in your own bed. Now, try not to burn down Uncle Liam's house while I'm at work, and keep the cursing to a minimum."

Gunnar looked sideways at Liam. Liam pasted on his most innocent of smiles. His family was insane. There was nothing to be done for it. Best Gunnar get used to it now if he planned on hanging around.

"Welcome to the family," Bree said, heading for the door with Liam in her wake. He reached past her and held it open for her. "Kill me now," she added under her breath for Liam's ears alone.

"Love you too," Liam assured her before closing the door behind her.

When Liam faced the room once more, Gunnar held Dakota. Liam kept his mouth from falling open by force of will alone. Judging by the uncomfortable expression Gunnar wore, Dakota had come to him. She was showing off her coloring sheet while talking his ear off about some rabbit Bree hit with her car. Liam bit his lip to keep from smiling. It was a battle. Gunnar glanced his way, catching Liam watching them. The smile won. Gunnar winked and went back to listening to Dakota. She was too big for anyone to be carrying around, but Gunnar was a big guy, and he wasn't complaining. Of course, if Dakota kept up the constant chatter, Gunnar might run for the hills soon. If so, it was better for Liam to know it now rather than later.

Four hours later, Gunnar was still there, and Liam found himself staring at Gunnar for longer periods of time. He could lose his heart to this man so freaking easily it was ridiculous. That idea was scary as hell, but Gunnar stayed put and helped out with everything. Cooking, cleaning, and keeping up with the kids. He didn't once lose his patience or look bored. While Kaz had always played with the girls when they came over, he'd made it clear he knew he could leave at any time. They were Liam's responsibility, and it was true, they were. Gunnar didn't make Liam feel alone in any way. He acted as if as long the girls were there, he would be too. Liam was fascinated by the phenomena.

They didn't get a single adult word in until both the girls went down for a nap. To keep from pouncing on him like a crazed fiend, Liam searched for a safe topic as he scrubbed crayon from the countertop.

"Whatever happened with that championship fight you were thinking of accepting?"

"I turned it down," Gunnar said right away, surprising Liam. "After giving it some real thought, I realized I don't want it. For the past two years, I've been passing on every challenge, thinking I wouldn't give," Gunnar paused and eyed the girls camped out on the couch for a second, as if making sure they were asleep, before continuing, "Wouldn't give the bastard the satisfaction."

"They're asleep, but these girls have heard much worse. They belong to my sister," Liam reminded Gunnar.

Gunnar shrugged. "I wasn't sure, but anyhow, this time, I really thought about everything you said, and questioned my reasons for always saying no. In the end, I realized it wasn't facing him I was backing down from. It's all about me. I don't want to be champion."

Liam smiled, proud of Gunnar for some reason he couldn't explain. "As long as you're doing it for you, then I'll always proudly stand behind you."

"That's all I've ever wanted."

Liam barely stopped himself from throwing the wet rag at Gunnar. "You're so full of shit."

"No, seriously," Gunnar argued. "Taking that challenge would've only been about showing him up or proving a point to myself. It wouldn't have anything to do with having the life I want or making you happy," he added with a wink. Even though Liam was certain Gunnar was blowing smoke up his ass, his heart still skipped a beat. To keep from showing it, he tried keeping the conversation rolling.

"What do you want out of life?"

Gunnar shrugged. "To be happy, I guess. Beyond that, I don't know. I've been waiting to accomplish the first part before thinking about the rest."

Liam realized he'd stopped cleaning to focus on Gunnar and hadn't moved since they'd started this conversation. Even after realizing it, he didn't move. He needed to hear every word coming from Gunnar's mouth. This conversation felt important for some reason he couldn't name. "You make it sound as if you've never been happy."

Gunnar leaned into the broom between his hands and focused on Liam. "I'm happy right now."

Liam's cheeks ached as his grin grew. "Awesome. I'll try to keep you that way."

"You don't have to try," Gunnar said, going back to sweeping. It was funny. Gunnar hadn't looked at him as he'd made his claim, but Liam believed Gunnar meant every word. Liam had meant his too. He would do everything in his power to keep Gunnar happy because he made him want to do so.

# Chapter Six

LIAM: *Do you have plans for Thanksgiving?*

Gunnar: *No. Since Mom died, I usually just go to the gym.*

Liam: *It's Bree's turn to cook. Would you like to join us?*

Gunnar: *Yes, but I don't want to intrude.*

Liam: *You'd better. Bree might find you if you don't accept.*

Gunnar: *What about you?*

Liam: *She already knows where to find me.*

Gunnar: *You know what I meant.*

Liam: *Yeah, I already know where to find you. I suggest you accept gracefully.*

Gunnar: *Anything, if it means seeing you.*

Liam: *Now that's what I call gracefully.*

---

Gunnar: *Since we're always together— thank God—we should get a Christmas tree together.*

Liam: *Real or fake?*

Gunnar: *Whatever you'd like. I've never had one and have no preference.*

Liam: *Never?*

Gunnar: *Never.*

Liam: *We'll remedy that tomorrow.*

---

Gunnar: *I hate that you're working. It's Valentine's Day.*

Liam: *We cater to the lonely.*

Gunnar: *I'm lonely.*

Liam: *Then come see me. There's no reason you can't visit me at work.*

Gunnar: *No thanks. It's nothing against what you do, but I don't want to watch while other men drool over you all night.*

Liam: *They might drool over me, but you're the only who gets to drool on me.*

Gunnar: *True. You can tie a ribbon around your dick when you get home, and I'll take you up on that offer.*

Liam: *Deal.*

Liam: *How did your fight go?*

Gunnar: *Fine. I won. Afterward was a nightmare.*

Liam: *You always win. You're you. What happened afterward?*

Gunnar: *There's some huge sports convention happening in the hotel where I'm staying. Someone recognized me, and I almost didn't make it back to the room with my skin intact.*

Liam: *It's tough being famous.*

Gunnar: *Whatever.*

Liam: *Ha. Miss you.*

Gunnar: *Miss you too, baby.*

---

Gunnar: *I SEE YOU GAVE MY NUMBER TO your sister.*

Liam: *Yeah. She wants you to help her plan my not-surprise birthday party.*

Gunnar: *She's not exactly subtle, is she?*

Liam: *Nope, but she's mine.*

Gunnar: *Are you sure? I think your parents should check.*

Liam: *LOL!*

Gunnar: *I hope you really laughed. You know I love your family. So, what do you want for your birthday? I want your surprise party to be perfect.*

Liam: *Just you.*

Gunnar: *You already have me.*

Liam: *Good, then it'll be the best birthday in history.*

---

SEVEN MONTHS OF BEING WITH GUNNAR went beyond description. Every day, Liam waited with bated breath, wondering if it would hold. As much as he'd like to believe his break with Kaz hadn't screwed him up a little, Liam realized it had. Several times, he'd caught himself staring at Gunnar, wondering. Were they the fighter and the stripper? Liam knew he couldn't do this job forever. One day, he'd be something else. But for now, anyone he dated would be forced to accept him like this. With Gunnar, every day it became a harder pill to swallow. Did Gunnar want him to quit? Maybe Liam was slowly destroying the best thing that ever happened to him and he didn't even realize it. Each day, Liam fell a little more for Gunnar. It was scary as hell how easily they'd slipped into always being together. The idea of losing Gunnar was twice as terrifying as anything he'd ever dealt with before.

At work, Liam more or less went through the motions. He did his number, fulfilled some lap dances, and took pictures with people who'd long past had enough to drink. His mind stayed firmly locked with Gunnar every second. More specifically, he kept reliving their kiss as Gunnar had dropped him off earlier. It was possible Liam searched for things that weren't there, but it had seemed different somehow. There'd been promise in Gunnar's touch. Or maybe, he just needed there to be hope for the future.

"Would you sit with me?"

Liam pasted on his usual friendly smile and pushed Gunnar from his mind before turning to greet his latest customer. He was a Viking. That was the first thought that popped into Liam's head the moment he set eyes on the man. Liam knew this game.

"If you'd like." Some people preferred conversation over dancing, especially this late at night when the crowd had thinned. Since it gave Liam a break and people tended to tip better for company than they did for lap dances, Liam couldn't complain. Liam moved to the man's table, joining the giant blond.

"I'm Boston," the Viking said the moment Liam settled in across from him.

Liam accepted his outstretched hand. "It's nice to meet you, Boston. You don't sound like you're from there."

Boston's eyes flashed with humor. "No. I was conceived there, but New Orleans is my home."

"Are you visiting Miami for business or pleasure?"

Boston's gaze never wavered from Liam's face. It was a nice change. "A little of both, I suppose. I'm actually staying in the Keys, but Miami has what I'm searching for, you know. You never gave me your name."

In the eight years Liam had worked for Fusion X, he'd gotten good at reading people. There was something about Boston. Liam couldn't quite put his finger on it, but he had a good handle on the rest of the man's intentions.

"You don't strike me as the type who likes to be lied to."

"You're right," Boston said, sounding overly serious.

Liam flashed his sweetest smile, hoping to thaw him. "Then you don't want me to answer that question."

Boston looked curious. "You never hand out your real name?"

Liam shook his head. "Never. House rules."

Boston set his elbow on the table before resting his chin in his palm. The man had great eyes. Somehow, Boston's stare made Liam feel as if they were alone. "That's okay. How about I order both of us a drink? You can keep me company, and I'll walk away feeling as if I spent my evening with a sexy stranger."

Liam experienced the oddest desire to blush. In his profession, he hadn't done that in years. Boston was incredibly sexy—too much so to be wasting his night paying for company. Something about the man reminded Liam of Gunnar. That thought brought Liam back to reality and cooled his heated skin.

"I get off in an hour, and I have to drive home." It was a complete lie. Gunnar had driven him to work, but Liam wasn't much of a drinker. Plus, unlike a lot of the dancers, he didn't drink on the job. "You can still order a drink if you'd like. I'll get some water and keep you company."

Boston didn't miss a beat. "Or—just hear me out —I could order you a drink and then drive you home, ensuring you arrive safe and sound." As Boston spoke, his smile grew, showing off perfect white teeth and a gorgeous smile. The mixture of innocence and wickedness bleeding from Boston's pores had Liam chuckling against his will.

"You are a tempting man," Liam admitted. "But I'm rather attached to this job, and—"

"House rules," Boston finished before Liam had the chance.

Liam nodded. "House rules. If you'd like, I could point out a couple of men who aren't as attached to this job."

Boston shook his head. "Now that we've met, no one else will do. I guess I'll have to go back to my room—sober and alone." Boston sounded so put out, Liam couldn't stop smiling. "You know," Boston added, turning playful. "We could always pretend you're the customer and I'm the dancer." Boston stood, towering over Liam as he moved closer. "Maybe I don't care so much about this job," he said as his hips moved to the beat of the music. Liam's cheeks ached. He was rarely surprised by anything. Sometimes, he thought he'd seen it all. Liam could honestly say no one had ever paid to give him a lap dance before. Boston had some moves, considering his inhuman size. It struck Liam—that was why Boston reminded him of

Gunnar. They had the same build—muscle and height.

"What do you say?" Boston asked, hovering over Liam while damn near sitting in his lap.

"Yeah," he said, drawing out the word. "I don't think my boss will accept role play as an excuse."

Boston sighed. "That's too bad. We could've made a great pair. I suppose if I have to leave here alone, I'd better do it now before I get too attached." He held out a folded up bill to Liam. "It was nice meeting you."

Liam pushed the money away and stood. "It was nice meeting you too, Boston." He took a step away before a hint of recklessness rose inside him. At the last second, he paused. "It's Liam, by the way." The smile exploding across Boston's face made breaking the rules worthwhile. It wasn't often he met nice people.

Watching Liam move toward him as Gunnar leaned against his car, waiting, felt like déjà vu. Unlike all those years ago when he'd met Liam after work, this time, Liam would be leaving with him. The way Liam smiled, as if he was overjoyed to see Gunnar, made Gunnar's heart turn over in his chest. He thought to tell Liam how sexy he looked, even after being on his feet for hours. Instead, as Gunnar's palms slid across Liam's hips, Liam's eyes fell closed and Gunnar's mind went blank. Nothing mattered except tasting Liam.

The instant their lips met, the air stuttered from Gunnar's lungs. Neither of them attempted to deepen the kiss. The breath leaving Liam was enough to sustain Gunnar. The knowledge prompted his confession.

"I missed you."

Liam's arms encircled Gunnar's neck. "It's only been a few hours."

"Doesn't matter."

At Gunnar's quick retort, Liam smiled. "Good, because I missed you too."

He had it so bad for this man. "You should get in the car. I want you all to myself for every possible second."

Liam didn't budge. "What did you do with your night?"

Gunnar growled and opened his mouth to beg Liam if need be. Liam's low chuckle rolled over Gunnar's skin a split-second before Liam covered Gunnar's mouth with his. It was quick and hard, but when Liam pulled away, Gunnar was panting. He swiped the moisture from Gunnar's bottom lip.

"We're already together, but I feel the same. I love being selfish and having you to myself."

Another car pulled from the parking lot, momentarily blinding Gunnar and catching his attention. He couldn't make out the driver, but something about his outline niggled at the back of Gunnar's mind.

"I'm in desperate need of a shower. Want to join me?"

Liam made the offer as he moved to climb into the truck. It pulled Gunnar's focus back his way. Gunnar's growing erection had him ready to agree to whatever Liam suggested. He jumped behind the wheel.

"I'm a big guy. It makes me an unintentional water hog or did you not notice from our last shower together?"

Liam's eyes flashed with humor. "Is that a no? I don't think you've ever turned me down before. Are you getting bored with me?"

Gunnar shifted into drive. "Hell no. I'm modifying your suggestion. How do you feel about a tub filled with hot water, bubbles, and me?"

"I feel like, judging by the size of your tub, this is something I'll need to sit in your lap for."

An evil smile tugged at Gunnar's lips. "I feel like we're on the same page."

"You never answered my question. What did you do with your night?"

"I went to the gym. Played with your nieces."

"What?" Liam asked. Laughter laced his question. "You played with my nieces? How did that come about?"

Gunnar glanced Liam's way and winked. "Bree stopped by to drop off a birthday invite for Willa's party in two weeks. She had the girls with her, and they stayed a good two hours. We had fun. The house is a mess," he added with a chuckle. Willa and Dakota were complete opposites, but Gunnar had easily fallen in love with them equally. He understood how they'd changed Liam's life and made him want more for himself.

"That I can believe. Willa is a hurricane."

"Actually, it's my fault," Gunnar admitted. "Dakota was crying because Bree told her she couldn't stay the night. I tore the house apart, making a fort for her while she was there. I told her time moved faster in my forts, so she actually did spend the night. It just went by really fast." Gunnar chuckled at his own story. Not because it was funny, but because the look on Bree's face had been priceless. They both knew Dakota wouldn't go to sleep when they got home because Gunnar had told her the night had already come and gone. It was such a cruel thing to do, but it made Dakota happy.

"You know she probably gave Bree hell after they left."

An evil laugh left Gunnar's lips before he could call it back. "Probably."

"You're so sexy right now. I really want you to take off your pants."

Gunnar cast a quick glance Liam's way at the claim. He was turned sideways in his seat, staring at Gunnar. Gunnar's mouth went dry. "Damn, why do you have to work in Miami? Fuck. Don't answer that. I know why. I'm sure it's more money than working a straight club, but it's an hour drive home, and the way you're looking at me…"

"You're rambling," Liam said, sounding sexy as sin while pointing out the obvious.

Gunnar nodded. After all, he couldn't claim otherwise. "You do that to me. I'm so ready to be inside you. While I was sitting in the parking lot, waiting for you to get off, I was thinking about us and missing you. I'm just ready to be home."

"You're still rambling," Liam said, unsnapping his seat belt while lifting the center console before moving closer. He cupped Gunnar's erection through his jeans. Gunnar sucked a deep breath in, trying to concentrate on driving. Liam increased the pressure on Gunnar's cock and bit his earlobe, making the job of getting them home safely even harder.

"Oh my God, Liam. You'll kill us if you keep this up."

"So pull over," Liam said, slipping down in the seat and working Gunnar's jeans loose. When Liam set Gunnar's erection free, immediately taking him down his throat, Gunnar hit the shoulder of the road. No way could he concentrate on driving with his dick in Liam's mouth.

"Fuck, Liam. I really don't want to go to jail tonight."

Liam pulled away, making sure he dragged his tongue up Gunnar's length as he went. "Then I suggest you keep an eye out for cops," Liam pointed out before taking Gunnar all the way down his throat once more.

Against his will, Gunnar's head fell back against the seat before he remembered he was supposed to be keeping an eye out. The way Liam's throat tightened and tugged at Gunnar's dick made it damn near impossible to think or see. His fingers found Liam's hair. His hips lifted, meeting Liam's mouth. It was out of his control. Liam could do things. Make him forget everything. Saliva rolled down his cock as hot lapping and tight suction pulled at his skin. The ecstasy of delicious pressure building from his balls and pushing against his crown couldn't be ignored. Liam didn't relent. No matter how demanding Gunnar became, Liam took it. He was so willing and talented. Dirty images of handcuffs, oils, candle wax, and hours of time on his hands flashed through Gunnar's mind. An hour drive would give him time to recover. Gunnar would fuck this man so hard when they got home. He would make Liam pay for this.

Sweat coated his brow as Gunnar strained toward release. His vision blurred before waves of intense pleasure overcame him. He swore his orgasm blinded him for a moment. It might've ended as quickly as it hit if not for Liam licking him clean. There was no man hotter than the one on his dick. He made Gunnar incapable of thinking of anyone else. Even after Liam moved back to his side of the truck and snapped his seat belt back in place, Gunnar couldn't tear his gaze away. Liam looked turned on.

Emotion welled inside Gunnar, threatening to overflow. "I—" Blue lights flashed behind his truck, tearing Gunnar from his confession. Horror raced through him as he quickly righted his clothes. When the policeman reached his door, Gunnar lowered his window.

The officer's flashlight hit Gunnar in the face. "Is everything okay here?"

Gunnar nodded. "Yeah. My check engine light came on. As soon as I pulled over, it went off again."

"License and proof of insurance, please."

Carefully avoiding Liam's gaze, in hopes of not laughing uncontrollably, Gunnar dug out his wallet and handed over his stuff. The policeman flashed his light over Gunnar's license before moving back to inspecting Gunnar's face. "Are you the same Gunnar Samson who fought Milo Wayne last month in Ft. Lauderdale?"

Gunnar nodded. "That's me."

A huge smile broke out across the other man's face. "That was a badass fight. I was in the third row. My wife got me tickets for our anniversary."

"Sounds like you have an awesome wife."

"I do," he said, passing Gunnar's stuff back over. "Man, I still can't believe you knocked out that big bastard in the first three minutes. I was almost pissed because I can't imagine what my wife paid for that ticket, but then I hit the casino and won six hundred bucks."

"Sounds like it was your lucky night." Gunnar was dying on the inside. He still hadn't come down from the high of Liam's blow job and this guy was talking about gambling. The moment seemed surreal.

The cop let out a loud bark of laughter. "It sure was, especially after I got home. Well, I'm glad your truck seems to be running fine. I suggest you get off this shoulder before you get hit. Have a great night." He started to walk away before pausing. "Oh, can I get your autograph? My wife won't believe this."

Gunnar smiled, willing to do anything to make this end. "Of course."

After scratching out a quick autograph, Gunnar watched the cop walk back to his car before the laughter hit. He glanced Liam's way, finding him with both hands over his face. A horrified-sounding snort came from behind his hands. Gunnar laughed harder at the sound.

Liam dropped his hands and met Gunnar's gaze. His eyes shone with humor.

"That was fun."

At Liam's claim, Gunnar laughed until his stomach ached. He was so in love with this man. No doubt, this craziness would be the rest of his life. Gunnar couldn't wait.

# Chapter Seven

THE SOUND of water splashing over the edge of Gunnar's tub, hitting the floor in time with every single one of Gunnar's moans, still rang in Liam's ears. The tips ran higher tonight than they had in a long time, and Liam knew the reason. His smile radiated happiness. He'd dreaded the idea of coming to work tonight. Every muscle in his body ached in the most delicious way. Gunnar was a nightly workout Liam was unaccustomed to experiencing. He hoped it never ended.

"Since you're obviously not a drinker, a vanilla shake should do the trick."

Liam stared down at the cup and straw in front of him, wondering what the hell. Following the arm holding it, Liam found his Viking, smiling like an idiot. "How did you get that in here?"

"People always let me have my way," Boston said, making Liam wonder if there was a double meaning hidden somewhere in his statement. Boston shook the cup at Liam since he still hadn't accepted it. "Are you planning to let my efforts go to waste?"

Liam eyed the cup suspiciously. "No offense, Boston, but I don't accept drinks from strangers."

"Oh, dang. I worried that might be the case." He stabbed the straw through the hole in the lid. "Guess I'll have to drink it. Will you sit with me for a little while anyhow?" Boston took a sip of the milkshake, making Liam feel like an ass.

Liam moved to the nearest empty table, hyper-aware of Boston's presence at his back. Once they were seated, Liam focused on Boston. "What brings you in again tonight?"

Boston took another swig of the shake before setting it aside. "You mean besides trying to win you over with delicious ice cream?"

In spite of himself, Liam chuckled. "Yeah, besides that."

One of Boston's massive shoulders rose in a half shrug. "I didn't care to sit in my hotel room alone."

"How much longer will you be in town?"

"A while," Boston answered evasively. "I have some business to settle before I can head back home. There's no real timeline. I'm here until it's done."

That piqued Liam's curiosity. "What kind of work do you do?"

"It's personal business," Boston said, sounding sad. "Not work related."

"Oh."

"My ex," Boston added.

"Oh," Liam repeated, for lack of anything more.

An overly bright smile stretched Boston's lips. "That was depressing. Tell me something about yourself while I wash the bitterness from my mouth." Boston lifted the shake to his lips as if intending to do just that.

"What would you like to know?"

"Tell me all about who owns your heart, since it's obviously not up for grabs."

The grin pulling at the corners of Liam's mouth was out of his control. Boston was right. It was funny everyone could see it. "His name is Gunnar."

"That's unusual."

"Says someone named Boston," Liam pointed out.

Boston shrugged. "Fair enough. What does Gunnar do for a living and why isn't he here, dogging your steps and giving everyone the evil eye?"

"He's a professional boxer, and I guess he trusts me."

A low whistle left Boston's lips. "A boxer, huh? I guess I'd better watch my step. Also, I'd say his trust isn't misplaced. I have ice cream and couldn't lure you into my big white van."

A snort escaped Liam. "Do you have a big white van?"

Boston's good humor was catching. "Metaphorically speaking, of course."

"Of course," Liam agreed. He didn't know what it was about Boston, but Liam liked him. It made a night of working pass a lot quicker than usual.

GUNNAR: *I HAD YOU A KEY MADE, AND I USED the one you gave me for the first time. I left your key on the end table right inside your front door. I hope you choose to use it sometime soon.*

As Gunnar promised, the key to his apartment sat waiting on the end table by the door. It wasn't the only thing. The smile stretching Liam's lips matched the one in his chest. A dozen long-stem roses sat next to the key along with a note. Liam bit his bottom lip, trying to squelch his grin as he flipped open the note. It wasn't happening. His happiness grew with every passing second.

*Liam,*

*I never thought to ask about your favorite flower. I grabbed these, thinking it might be romantic. Now, I worry you won't like them. I hate that I just got back into town and have to leave again in a few days. Miss you like crazy.*

*Anyhow, now you have a key and can come and go as you please. I hope you had a good night at work. Don't hate me if you have some crazy flower allergy. – Gunnar*

Liam's eyes burned. Maybe some people thought flowers were a cliché gift. No one had ever bought them for Liam before. In his apartment, late at night, and where no one could see, Liam admitted the truth to himself. He was in love with Gunnar. Some days, it was the simplest thing in the world. Other days, Liam remembered all the dreams he'd had before Gunnar came along. He still wanted each one to come true. The problem was, he didn't know if Gunnar was looking for the same things out of life. Liam couldn't withstand losing someone else because he couldn't part with his dream of a normal life. The idea of Gunnar saying he didn't see them settling down damn near crippled Liam just thinking about it.

For five minutes, Liam stared at Gunnar's key and debated. All he needed to do was climb into bed, and it would be morning. He could run downstairs and be with Gunnar. Those few hours felt so far away. Incapable of standing it another second, Liam jogged for the bedroom. He ran through the motions of getting ready for bed. After slipping on a pair of pajama pants, Liam snagged Gunnar's key and headed downstairs.

Darkness and the hum of the air conditioner met Liam as he crept inside Liam's apartment. With the door locked behind him, Liam snuck through the house, doing his best not to wake Gunnar or trip over Loki. While straining to see if Gunnar was sleeping, Liam slipped out of his pants. If Gunnar snored, Liam never noticed, and he wasn't hearing it now. He eased into bed beside Gunnar, relieved to simply be close to the man filling his heart. There was no way Liam could've waited until morning to smell Gunnar's skin. He needed this man too much. The instant Liam settled down at Gunnar's side, Gunnar rolled, trapping Liam on his stomach and beneath Gunnar's large frame.

"I hoped you'd show up," Gunnar said before licking Liam's ear.

Liam's body's reaction was swift and severe. His hard-on was on the verge of painful. "Couldn't stay away," Liam said, pushing the words past his barely inflating lungs. Sometimes he wondered if Gunnar realized how much bigger he was than Liam. Not that Liam cared. Oxygen was overrated anyhow. The erection digging into Liam's ass made it all worthwhile.

Gunnar's short fingernails scraped Liam's hip as he dragged Liam's boxers down one hip. "I've been thinking about you," Gunnar admitted as he shoved Liam's underwear all the way down. "Now I'm horny as hell. Being inside you is all I can think about right now. Your tight heat squeezing me," Gunnar said, kneeing Liam's legs apart. "The way you moan when I stretch you wide," Gunnar added as he swiped the head of his cock across Liam's asshole, torturing him. He probed at Liam's ass.

Liam clasped the sheets, tasting blood as he bit his lip to keep from begging. "Condom," he reminded Gunnar.

Gunnar froze. "Fuck. You make me forget myself. All I can think about is the way my chest feels when we're connected."

Something inside Liam gave way. "I don't even care about the condom. Just fuck me, Gunnar. I need you inside me."

Chill bumps raced down Liam's back as Gunnar's lips brushed Liam's nape. "Is that what you want, baby? I'm clean, but I want to you to feel safe."

There was a real danger of Liam cracking a tooth when Gunnar's lips moved lower. The torment was real. "I'm clean too, and I want you inside me now. Please?" So much for not begging. Pride flew out the window. The sensation of Gunnar's hard body pressing against Liam's had Liam's brain misfiring. There was enough electricity between them to power an entire city. It had always been that way. They were molten.

Gunnar pressed inside an inch before retreating. A low moan escaped Liam. At the sound, Gunnar bit into Liam's shoulder and dipped farther inside. With nothing except Gunnar's pre-cum lubricating the way, the sting added to the list of sensations driving Liam insane. Liam rocked his hips, grinding his erection against the mattress. He needed more.

"No more playing, please, Gunnar. I need you to fuck me."

At his plea, Gunnar impaled Liam with his cock. A cry tore from Liam's throat. His dick leaked. While clinging to Liam's hips, Gunnar drove home again, holding Liam in place and giving Liam the hard ride he'd been seeking.

"Oh my God, Liam. You feel like Heaven on my cock. You're so hot and tight. I want to stay here for the rest of the night." He slowed, as if he planned to do just that. A cry of denial left Liam, but Gunnar didn't relent. "I wonder how long you'll let me torture you. Is your dick crying, Liam? Are my sheets soaked yet?" Words passed Liam's lips, muffled by the mattress and beyond Liam's understanding. The only sense still working for him was his ability to feel. Gunnar changed angles, hitting that awesome spot Liam loved so much. Liam's fingers ached from gripping the sheet too tight. "Is the pressure beating at the head of your cock, making it beg for the slightest tickle to release it? What if I put my tongue—"

An orgasm ripped through Liam, taking away Liam's ability to hear whatever Gunnar was saying. Gunnar's name left Liam's lips on a cry, reverberating from the walls. Something between a pant and a grunt brushed the shell of Liam's ear as Gunnar lost control.

"Oh, fuck, Liam. Helpless against you," he breathed against Liam's neck, stealing Liam's heart. Between Gunnar's massive weight, Liam's breath-stealing orgasm, and the love sitting on Liam's windpipe, Liam wondered if he would pass out. When Gunnar rolled to the side, Liam sucked in a deep pull of oxygen even as he rolled with Gunnar. Cool air hit Liam's stomach, reminding him of the mess they'd made.

"Fuck. I don't want to move, but there's cum all over the bed."

A low chuckle brushed Liam's ear. "See? This is why we can't have nice things. We're too gooey together."

Happiness and a bit of delirium had Liam's stomach shaking with laughter. "You make us sound like candy."

"Hell yeah," Gunnar said, shifting to his feet and heading for the bathroom. "We're sweet as hell together."

Liam stared at Gunnar's back, speechless. There was only one thought in his head. He fucking loved this man.

---

A LIGHT GRAY SKY STREAKED WITH FINGERS of orange greeted Gunnar as he headed for his truck. A warm breeze kissed his skin and smelled of the ocean even from miles away. He loved the early morning, but he hated leaving Liam. If Liam hadn't needed sleep after working late and Gunnar keeping him up half the night, Gunnar might've dragged the man from the bed just to keep him company at the gym. No doubt, Liam had become a sickness for Gunnar.

Inside his truck, he stared at the door of his apartment. The sting of Liam's goodbye kiss still lingered on Gunnar's lips. He could go back inside. No one would judge him other than Aden. He could text Aden now and let him know he wasn't coming. It was just that easy. In a matter of seconds, Gunnar could be back beneath the covers with Liam—where he belonged.

Gunnar felt for his phone. It wasn't there. A smile stretched his lips. Seemed it was serendipitous. He was meant to stay home. While jogging for the door, Gunnar searched for his house key. Before he could get the key in the lock, the door flew open and Liam appeared. Gunnar's ridiculous heart skipped a beat at the sight of Liam's sleep-mussed dirty blond hair and tired smile.

"I forgot my phone."

Liam's sexy smile grew. It was brilliant as if he was overjoyed to see Gunnar even though he'd just kissed the man goodbye. That shit was more addictive than crack.

"I was just coming to get you. It chirped the moment the door closed behind you."

Gunnar held Liam's gaze as he passed the phone over. His heart raced as if they hadn't seen each other in days. This man had him tied up in knots. There was no denying Liam's power over him.

"Someone saved as TFB texted you," Liam said, pulling Gunnar from the fantasy of dropping to his knees right there. It was the same as an ice bucket to the face. Not the ice. The whole fucking, cold-ass metal bucket.

"Fucking bastard."

A surprised-sounding snort left Liam. "Gee, thanks."

"Not you," Gunnar said, immediately feeling like shit. "TFB. That's what TFB stands for—The Fucking Bastard. It's my ex." Even using an acronym, saying those words was like chewing on broken glass for Gunnar. Liam didn't seem shocked nor did he respond. Gunnar checked the message.

TFB: *What is this shit about you refusing my challenge again?*

Gunnar growled. Hatred filled his heart to the brim. Without a single thought, he shot off a response.

Gunnar: *Don't text me again.*

TFB: *If you don't want me texting you, then answer my question.*

Gunnar: *Fuck off, dick head.*

Powering down his phone, Gunnar shoved the device in his back pocket because he just couldn't deal. There was no such thing as enough time or distance to satisfy Gunnar's rage toward the man who'd destroyed his life. All it had taken was two messages from his ex, and the world looked black.

He shoved aside his bitterness. Gunnar focused on Liam, hoping to wash the bad taste from his mouth. "Sorry you were exposed to that." He took a step closer to Liam. A wicked glint entered Liam's eyes, and Gunnar took another step in the man's direction. Liam reached up and encircled Gunnar's neck. Gunnar kept crowding Liam's space, needing his goodness to wipe away the taint.

"I like it when you expose things to me. You should hurry back from your gym session and expose yourself some more."

Gunnar moved another inch closer, walking Liam backward. Once he cleared the doorway, he kicked the door closed behind them. "Maybe I could show you something right now."

"You have a training session scheduled." The humor in Liam's voice made Gunnar smile and his anger disappear.

"It was endurance training day. You could always help me out with that."

Liam's palms flattened against Gunnar's chest.

Gunnar automatically flexed.

Liam hummed in the back of his throat. "I don't know if I'm up to the challenge. You're feeling a bit out of shape."

A surprised chuckle left Gunnar's lips. It sounded evil, even to his ears. "Is that so?" Without giving Liam a chance to get away, Gunnar swept him off his feet and headed for the bedroom. Liam's roar of laughter filled Gunnar's ears and heart.

"You'll make Aden hate me if you skip out on him because of me."

Gunnar didn't slow. "Nope. You've challenged my manhood. Now you must pay."

"Mmm, you're right. I need to be punished."

Liam's eyes shone with humor, making Gunnar question his seriousness. When he reached the edge of the bed, Gunnar didn't toss Liam onto it, as he'd planned. Instead, he froze. Gunnar stared down at the man in his arms. A rush of intense emotions overcame him.

Liam's smile fell. "Sometimes you terrify me."

The confession floored Gunnar to the point he couldn't respond. Never in a million years would he hurt Liam in any way. He was speechless. Liam's hold on Gunnar's neck tightened.

"That came out wrong," Liam said, looking every bit as scared as he claimed. "I meant, sometimes the way you make me feel terrifies me. Sometimes, I think, what if he leaves and doesn't come back?" Liam visibly swallowed. "That's scary, because I think I'd be willing to give up every dream I've had and replace it with you."

Yes. Gunnar knew exactly what Liam meant. If anyone asked him to explain how he felt about Liam, those were the words he would've chosen. He eased Liam onto the mattress before climbing on top of him and settling down with his ear pressed to Liam's chest. He needed to hear Liam's heart beating. Liam's arms encircled Gunnar, holding him in place. Gunnar tested a thousand confessions before discarding each one as weak. When Gunnar had been dating Boston, he had given Gunnar all the words Gunnar wanted to hear, and still he'd leveled Gunnar's life. Words meant nothing. Liam deserved actions.

"What are your plans for Monday?"

Liam ran his fingers through Gunnar's hair as he answered. "Nothing."

"Good," Gunnar said before pressing his lips to the center of Liam's chest and meeting his gaze. "I'll be out of town this weekend for the fight in Dallas and won't be home until late Sunday night. First thing Monday, we should move your things downstairs. That is, until we can find a house."

Liam's fingers froze halfway through another stroke of Gunnar's scalp. He felt Liam's breathing stop. Smoky blue eyes searched Gunnar's face, as if assessing his seriousness.

Gunnar made damn sure every ounce of his earnestness showed in his gaze. He loved this man. Whatever dream Liam wanted, Gunnar needed to give it to him.

Liam went back to playing with Gunnar's hair. "Okay."

With one word, Liam gave Gunnar the entire world.

# Chapter Eight

"So, I thought things over last night and have come to the conclusion that you must be a chocolate lover."

Liam glanced down at the cup Boston held out to him. In spite of himself, a huge grin spread across his face. He felt it happen, but it was out of his control. "I hate to keep being this person, but you know I can't accept that."

Boston sighed. "That's what I thought." Just as he had the night before, Boston took a drink. "I guess I'll work on getting fat by myself again, and maybe you can stop by my table for a visit before the end of the night."

"Maybe so," Liam agreed. With a wink, he left Boston alone with his shake. He still had two stage performances left, and he couldn't hang out with Boston all night. By the time he found Boston again, two hours had passed.

He pushed a new cup Liam's way. "So strawberry must be your thing."

Against his will, a snort of laughter left Liam. "Where did this one come from? Did you leave and come back?"

"Nope. A man needs to have some secrets." Boston's blue eyes shone with laughter as he made the claim. Knowing he'd hate himself for it, Liam stabbed the straw through the lid. Even as he took his first sip, Liam questioned his sanity. "Ha," Boston crowed with satisfaction. "It may have taken me a few weeks of dogged determination, but I knew I'd win you over eventually."

Liam shook his head. "If I wake up tomorrow in a tub full of ice and missing a kidney, I'll never forgive you."

Boston's smile grew. "I'm not after your kidneys."

"What are you after?" The question left Liam's lips before he could call it back. He didn't back down. Boston did want something. Liam just hadn't figured out the man's game yet.

The other man's expression shifted, and Liam saw a different side of Boston. For a full minute, Boston didn't respond. When he did, he sounded resigned. "I'm not sure. I'll let you know when I figure it out."

"Fair enough," Liam agreed. He could enjoy an hour of Boston's company without knowing all his motives, and he did.

EXHAUSTION WEIGHED ON LIAM'S shoulders as he headed outside after his shift. It was only Friday and Liam already wondered how he'd make it through another night of working. The fact that Gunnar wouldn't be home until Sunday made things worse. It seemed like Gunnar had been traveling more and more often lately. He'd given Liam an open invitation to come along anytime he liked, but like everyone else in the world, Liam had to work.

Liam reached to open his car door. He froze as he caught sight of his front tire. It was flat. The invisible weight sitting on his shoulders increased. Switching directions, he headed for his trunk, intent on retrieving his spare. His gaze landed on his back tire. It was flat too. He barely stopped himself from stamping his feet, the way Willa always did during a fit. Circling his car, he checked the rest of his tires, finding they were okay. It didn't change anything. He was still screwed since he only had one spare.

Not to mention, it was two in the morning and he didn't have anyone to call. Bree couldn't leave her kids alone to come get him. His parents kept their ringer turned off at night—not that they would hear it anyhow. With Gunnar out of town, Liam had one option—Kaz. Merge didn't close until three. If Liam was lucky, he could catch a ride home with his friend.

The door to Fusion X opened. Music spilled out along with a lone figure. A bad feeling overcame Liam when he recognized it was Boston. Liam wasn't sure why he was bothered. Boston hadn't given him a bad vibe inside the club, but for some reason, standing alone in the dark parking lot, Liam didn't feel right about the situation. Everything felt too convenient.

"Is everything okay?"

The moment Boston spoke, Liam's discomfort melted away. Liam waved toward his car. "My tires are flat."

Boston glanced down. "Dude," he said, dragging out the word. "Did you run over something on the way to work?"

Liam shrugged and swiped a hand across his face. "Who the fuck knows?"

"Want me to wait with you until your man gets here?"

In spite of his bad mood, a genuine smile tugged at Liam's lips at the mention of Gunnar. It was obvious Boston wasn't truly interested in Liam in a sexual way. It was a breath of fresh air when it came to meeting people at work.

"He's out of town this weekend."

Boston pulled a face. "That sucks. Do you need a ride home?"

Liam shook his head. No matter how nice Boston seemed, Liam wasn't stupid enough to get in the car with a stranger. "My friend works down at Merge. I'll walk over there and catch a ride home with him. Thanks for the offer, though." Liam thought that would be the end of it. Boston shifted from one foot to the other, looking unsure before glancing in Merge's direction.

"I'll walk with you."

Liam waved off his offer. "That's not necessary."

Boston's expression changed, hardening. "It's dark, and—no offense, but this isn't the best part of town. You're not making that walk alone. What if something happened to you? I'd have to live the rest of my life knowing I let you go alone."

Liam held his hands up in surrender. "All right. If it means that much to you."

With a smile that seemed a bit too triumphant, Boston fell into step beside Liam as he headed toward Merge. For five minutes, silence filled the air until Liam couldn't take it any longer. "Thank you for walking with me. Although, I have to point out, I used to make this walk every Wednesday, Friday, and Saturday night for three years without ever once being accosted."

Boston snorted. "That's because I wasn't here to accost you. Why did you make the walk three days a week for three years?" Boston asked before Liam could manage a retort to his accosting claim.

"My friend, Kaz, is also my ex."

Another minute of silence followed his confession before Boston spoke. "That's interesting. What does he do at Merge?"

Liam barely stopped himself from pointing out it wasn't the least bit interesting. "He's a bouncer."

From the corner of his eye, Liam saw Boston nod. "How's your man feel about you riding home with your ex?"

If Liam was being honest with himself, he wasn't entirely sure. Liam didn't hang out with Kaz often, and Gunnar had never said a word against Kaz, but Gunnar had a jealous streak that showed up at random times. It didn't make an appearance often, but there were instances when Liam got the impression Gunnar didn't care for what Liam did for a living. If he had a problem with strangers getting too close to Liam, spending too much time with an ex might be an issue. Liam got it. If Gunnar took his clothes off for anyone else or hung out with one of his exes, Liam would lose his shit. It might not be fair, but there it was.

"You're being awful quiet. Does that mean he wouldn't be too happy with you if he knew?"

"Under the circumstances, I'm sure he'd understand," Liam answered evasively.

A low chuckle left Boston's lips and crawled down Liam's spine, letting Liam know Boston wasn't fooled. "You deserve someone who'll be around to take care of you." Boston's voice turned sexy and cajoling. The bad feeling Liam experienced earlier came back with a vengeance.

Liam shook his head. "He has his job and I have mine," Liam said, barely hanging on to his temper. "Also, I'm not a child. I don't need anyone—much less someone to take care of me."

"It's one thing to be independent, but people weren't meant to be alone."

The edge of the building where Kaz worked came into view. Liam was beyond grateful, considering his level of irritation. "I'm here—safe and sound. You can leave me here. Like I said, I really appreciate you walking with me." Even to Liam's ears, he sounded overly bright.

Catching him off guard, Boston snagged Liam's sleeve and towed him toward a darkened alcove beside the building. Once out of sight, Boston faced off against him, looking furious. "It drives me batshit that you question every nice thing anyone does for you."

Liam's brows drew together in confusion in the face of Boston's anger. "Who says I do? You don't really know me."

"Are you denying it?"

He couldn't. As much as Liam hated how well this virtual stranger could read him, Liam couldn't call Boston a liar.

"See," Boston said when Liam didn't speak up in his own defense. "You should be with someone who gives you the confidence to be needy. When you trust no one, you lean on no one. You can tell me he's amazing and you're over-the-moon being with him, but I know the secret you're keeping when I look at you. In your heart, you expect he'll break you any day now. You're just waiting on that other shoe to drop." Liam wasn't quick enough, coming to Gunnar's defense, and Boston wasn't finished. "I don't know this guy. Hell, I don't know you all that well, but I know you don't think you're good enough to hang on to him, and that's such bullshit." He dug around in his pocket, coming out with a pen and card. Boston scratched something out on the card before shoving it in the front pocket of Liam's jeans. "Call me when he breaks your heart, and I'll show you what it's like to be with a real man."

Confusion and anger held Liam in place long after Boston walked away. Other than the first time they'd met, Liam hadn't gotten the impression Boston was truly interested in him. He'd talked a lot about his ex, and being in town, attempting to settle things with him. Liam had thought, erroneously it seemed, that Boston was looking for a friend. Now Liam worried he'd somehow led Boston on. Fuck. It had been a horrid night. All he wanted was to go home and crawl into bed. He should call a cab, but then he'd still have to wait forever.

Taking a deep breath, Liam circled the building to the door. Rather than stepping inside, he stood just outside the doorway until he spotted Kaz. He waved, snagging the man's attention. Kaz easily pushed his way through what was left of the crowd. The concern written on Kaz's face made Liam wonder what Kaz saw in Liam's expression.

"You okay?"

Another overwhelming wave of exhaustion hit Liam. He should've called a cab. Maybe Boston wasn't the only man who'd get the wrong impression. What if he unintentionally always gave Kaz hope by staying friends with him? Fuck. He needed sleep.

"Two of my tires are flat," Liam said, incapable of claiming he was okay. "I was hoping I could catch a ride home with you. If you've got plans after work, feel free to tell me to fuck off, and I'll call a cab."

The line between Kaz's brows deepened. "Are you fucking kidding? If you need help, that'll always come first with me." He glanced at his watch. "I've still got forty-five here. Do you want to come inside and get a drink or would you rather wait in the car?"

Liam could've hugged him. "If you don't mind, I'd rather wait in the car. I'm so goddamn tired."

Kaz eyed him with obvious concern as he dug his keys out and passed them over. "Is everything okay besides the tires? I can cut out early if you need me to."

Every claim Boston made about Liam rang through Liam's head. He pasted on a fake smile. "I'm good. Just tired."

Kaz glanced over his shoulder as if weighing his options before meeting Liam's stare once more. "I'll still try to cut out a few minutes early. Just go relax."

This time, the tug pulling at Liam's lips was real. Without a word, he headed for Kaz's car, sighing when he finally climbed inside.

Without a second's hesitation, Liam laid the seat back and closed his eyes.

---

AFTER TWO HOURS OF TEXTING LIAM without a response, Gunnar drove past his work. Liam's car sat in the parking lot with two flat tires. While the sight explained why Liam's car wasn't at the apartment, it didn't explain why Liam wasn't. Gunnar's worry exploded into full-blown panic. His phone rang as he pulled from the parking lot, and Gunnar damn near broke the thing in his race to answer.

His concern showed itself in way of fury. "Where the fuck are you?"

"Hey, baby," Liam answered, sounding exhausted and draining away Gunnar's panic.

He tried reeling his rage in. "Hey. Are you okay? I've been texting and calling for two hours. You've had me scared shitless."

Liam yawned. "Sorry, baby. When I got off work, my tires were flat, so I walked down to Merge to catch a ride with Kaz."

"So you're home," Gunnar said, damn near fainting in his relief.

"No. I'm at Kaz's. He still had an hour left on the clock when I got there, so I waited for him in the car and fell asleep. He decided to go on home since you're supposed to be out of town, and he knew I wouldn't have a way to get around tomorrow...or today, depending on how you look at it. Of course, I see from your texts that you're home early. What happened?"

"The fight was postponed because of a problem with the venue. I'd planned to surprise you, but you never came home. Jesus, Liam. You seriously scared me. Do you want me to come get you?"

"I'm sorry, baby. I didn't know you were home or I would've called you first. Now I'm too tired to budge. Damn, I hope I'm not coming down with something. Ever since I got off work, I'm having a hard time keeping my eyes open. When Kaz gets up, I'll have him bring me home. Until then, you need to get some rest."

Disappointment weighed heavily on Gunnar. He missed the hell out of Liam. He was tempted to drive to Kaz's and break down the door. Somehow, he called the temptation under control. "All right, darling. I miss you so much." The admission was out there before Gunnar knew he'd make it.

A noise came through the line. It sounded like Liam was content. "I miss you too, baby. Hopefully, Kaz won't sleep too late."

"If he does, call me. I'll come get you."

"Okay."

Damn, Gunnar was so in love with this man. He didn't want this conversation to end, but Liam sounded exhausted. "I guess I'd better let you get back to sleep."

"Okay," Liam repeated. "Gunnar," he said, stopping Gunnar from hanging up, "I'm serious about you getting some sleep. You'll need it."

The wickedness in Liam's claim had Gunnar's smile stretching wide enough to make his cheeks ache. "You too," Gunnar promised before disconnecting the call. He could wait a few more hours if it meant Liam getting enough sleep for him. Yep. That did sound like a solid plan.

Kaz slept much later than Liam would've like if he'd been awake to notice. After hanging up with Gunnar, Liam closed his eyes and died. Not literally, of course, but he definitely didn't remember a thing afterward until opening his eyes ten hours later. Kaz seemed to be in the same boat. He nodded blankly while Liam asked him to carry him home. Neither of them spoke on the drive to Liam's apartment.

Liam wasn't sure he would've said anything at all if not for the sight greeting him the moment his building came into view. Boston had Gunnar boxed in against the closed door of his apartment while Gunnar stood with both arms crossed over his chest, looking angrier than Liam had ever seen him.

"Oh my God. What is he doing here?"

Kaz squinted out the windshield at the man in question. "Who is that?"

"This guy, Boston," Liam answered with a shrug, and sounding more bitter than intended. "He came into my work one night a while back. At first, he seemed okay, but now I'm not so sure. You know I'm good at reading people. I haven't felt threatened or anything." Liam chewed on his bottom lip as he watched Boston get in Gunnar's face, wondering what was being said. "Damn. Looks like he's starting shit with Gunnar now. I feel sort of stalked. Why else would he be here?"

"Why didn't you say something before now?" Kaz roared, focusing on Liam, sounding more than a little pissed and cutting off his complaints. "I'll kill him."

Reaching over, Liam snagged Kaz's arm before he could jump from the vehicle. "Don't. Okay? I'll figure out what's going on and get rid of him. This is my fault for being too nice."

Kaz's features softened a hair. "You get that I love you, right?" Before Liam could respond or even absorb the rapid topic change, Kaz continued, "I should've married you long before you were forced to ask me. My only excuse is you scared the hell out of me. I'll never be more than I am, and I worried one day that wouldn't be enough. You'll never understand how sorry I am or how much it kills me being without you. Maybe I'm not worth much," he said, pushing Liam's hand away. "But I can do this for you."

Without giving Liam time to process or react, Kaz bounded from the car. Liam jumped out behind him in pursuit.

"Hey," Kaz called, announcing his arrival. "It's obvious the dude doesn't want you crowding his space," Kaz said, using his booming security voice. He reached for Boston's shoulder. The instant Kaz's palm collided with Boston's skin, Boston exploded. In a move almost too quick to see, the man spun and threw a right hook, catching Kaz in the center of his face. Kaz went down. Liam broke into a run, jumping into the fray before another blow landed. Everything moved at a rapid pace. Yet Liam still had time to contemplate all the ways he would die the moment these big motherfuckers started going at each other for real with him stuck in the middle.

"What the fuck is going on out here?" Liam yelled, hoping to be heard over the shouting. Mostly, it was Kaz's angry cursing.

Boston held his hands up, showing his surrender. "He snuck up on me."

"What the fuck ever," Liam grumbled, reaching past Gunnar and throwing open his front door. "Kaz, I'm sure Gunnar won't mind if you make yourself at home. Go clean up."

"I don't know what to say," Boston said, trying to help Kaz stand. Kaz swatted away his hands. "Truly," Boston added. "You caught me off guard and I overreacted."

Kaz kept his nose pinched, attempting to stem the blood flow. "You can tell it to my lawyer," Kaz spat as he brushed past Boston, heading inside.

Boston rubbed the spot between his eyes. "That's just fucking great."

His obvious aggravation only served to piss Liam off further. "You brought this on yourself, showing up at my job all the time, and now here."

"He came to your work?" The deadly growl in Gunnar's tone set Liam on edge.

"It's nothing," Liam said, choosing the bare minimum of truth.

Gunnar turned his fury Boston's way. "What the fuck, Boston? You think threatening Liam will get me to fight you, is that it? That's low, even for you."

Liam closed his eyes for a second as if it would make Gunnar's claim make sense. "Wait. What?"

"Oh, babe," Boston said, sounding strangely hurt. "Not everything is about you."

"What?" Liam repeated, because no one was listening to him.

Gunnar continued ignoring him. "I have to admit, fucking with Liam was a damn good strategy. If a fight is what you're after, it's what you'll get. Nobody fucks with mine. I accept your challenge for the cruiserweight championship. Did you get what you came for?"

Liam's mind went blank. Wasn't Gunnar's ex the cruiserweight champion? Wait. This was Gunnar's ex? Liam felt... he didn't even know how he felt. He'd kept his back to Gunnar, ready to stand with him against Boston, but this bullshit... wow. Liam didn't know what to think. Boston's gaze moved over Liam's face, as if searching for something Liam couldn't name.

"Is this really what you want?"

Gunnar's arms encircled Liam's waist, pulling him back against his chest before Liam could respond.

"No," Gunnar said, answering Boston's question. "This right here is what I have my heart set on. I want marriage, kids, and the white picket fence. The whole damn thing. You're the one who needed the championship to make your life complete. Unfortunately, you've made it more than clear I'm not allowed any happiness until I've put you back in your place—out of my life."

There was no way Gunnar couldn't feel Liam's heart pounding. The rapid beat sounded like gunfire in Liam's ears. Gunnar had used Liam's words. He wanted all the same things Liam did.

Boston rolled his eyes. "I wasn't fucking talking to you, Gunnar." He focused on Liam once more. "Is this what you want? I could give you so much more than Gunnar can. I was serious last night. You'd never wonder when the other shoe would drop." Gunnar's grip loosened on Liam's waist. "We have a connection," Boston added, motioning between them. "I know you've felt it too."

Gunnar's arms fell away. Liam wanted to snatch them back. He needed Gunnar to keep him safe from whatever was happening.

"What's he talking about?"

At Gunnar's question, Liam turned. The hurt shining in Gunnar's eyes matched his tone. Liam wanted to comfort him. With everyone watching, the only thing Liam could do was give Gunnar the truth.

"He's been to Fusion X a few times, and last night—when I came out to find my tires flat—Boston walked with me to Merge, making sure I got there safely." Liam felt certain there was more he could say to clear things away, but at the moment, his mind wouldn't function.

Boston moved to flank Liam. "You don't have to explain anything, Liam. You haven't done anything wrong. It's not like you have any control over where I turn up, and besides, the two of you aren't married."

Gunnar's gaze hardened. He didn't look away from Liam. "I guess I know now why you didn't answer my calls last night, or come home," he added, driving in the final nail.

It was a shot to the chest. Liam's mouth fell open. His shock complete. "I told you why I didn't answer your calls. While I was waiting for Kaz to get off work, I fell asleep. By the time I got your messages, I was still half asleep, and there was no sense in you coming to get me. Ask Kaz." Liam paused, stopping himself before dragging Kaz any further into things. This was bullshit. He'd spent part of the night trying to tell Boston how much Gunnar meant, and now here they were. "You know what. Never mind." Liam didn't know what the fuck was going on with Gunnar. It didn't matter. He knew the truth, but it was more than obvious by Gunnar's expression that he didn't believe Liam. No way in hell would Liam beg Gunnar to believe in him, especially with everyone staring at him.

Liam took a step away. "I'm not sure what sort of fucked up shit the two of you have going on between you, but I'm out."

Without meeting anyone's gaze, Liam headed for the stairs. He couldn't get away from Boston and Gunnar quick enough to suit his heart. Of all the jumbled thoughts racing through his mind, one stood out from the rest. He'd known Gunnar would break his heart, and so had Boston. How sad.

GUNNAR WATCHED LIAM TAKE THE STAIRS two at a time with Loki on his heels. The cat must've escaped while the door had been open. Funny how that detail stood out. Even Loki knew Gunnar was an ass and didn't want to stay with him. His chest ached. Everything hurt. That was what being near Boston always did to him. Now, it was a hundred times worse. Liam had been meeting up with Boston. Taking his clothes off for Boston. There was no bigger betrayal as far as Gunnar was concerned. Unfortunately, Boston was still standing there, eating up Liam with his gaze as Liam ran away with Gunnar's heart.

When Gunnar found his voice, it was filled with almost as much venom as his heart. "It's time for you to go. You got what you came for. Now get lost."

Boston tore his gaze away from Liam's door and focused on Gunnar. A half-smile played on his lips, making Gunnar itch to knock out his teeth.

"I didn't get what I came for. Not by a longshot. You know, you should really ask yourself what it is about you, making everyone you fall in love with leave you. Because, really, you're the only common factor."

Gunnar lunged. A vise-like grip tightened around his waist, holding him in place. The confusion Gunnar experienced over his in-ability to move gave Boston time to get away unscathed. A low chuckle followed Boston to his car.

"See you in the ring, Gunnar," Boston taunted, making Gunnar damn near lose his shit. When Boston was out of sight, the anchor weighing him down disappeared. Gunnar spun, finding a pissed off Kaz facing off against him.

"Fuck. I forgot you were here." Gunnar ran his hands through his hair, wanting to pull it out at the roots. "You're strong enough to hold me back but couldn't avoid a punch to the face. Idiot," Gunnar said, needing to lash out at someone.

Kaz's furious expression didn't abate. "I had my reasons for not avoiding his swing. Can you say the same?"

Confusion mixed with Gunnar's rage, making his brain slow. "What?"

Kaz made an impatient gesture. "That bastard just beat you down, and you let it happen for no reason other than you're a complete moron."

"What the fuck are you talking about?"

Kaz pushed past him, heading for the stairs. Before Kaz made it to the bottom, he reversed course, going nose to nose with Gunnar, as if both his eyes weren't already turning black.

"I should keep my mouth shut. After all, your loss could easily be my gain, but I can't. You just let the best thing that's ever happened to you walk away. I get it. You're obviously an insecure douche, and your ex has got you fucked in the head. But Liam, he's no cheat. What he is, is someone who does a job he hates, one that makes him feel cheap, because it's the fastest route to having the life he's always dreamed of having, and I made him feel like he's not good enough to do anything else. I just watched you take that insecurity I instilled and break him with it. Good luck fixing that, asshole."

This time, Kaz didn't look back as he headed up the stairs, going where Gunnar should—to comfort Liam. With nothing but anger and jealousy in his heart, Gunnar slammed the front door behind him. Fuck it. He was tired of dancing for men who didn't know how to be faithful while he gave them everything. Gunnar paced the floor, watching his feet, and ready to tear off his skin. Fucking Boston. The way he'd looked at Liam, as if he knew the way Liam tasted, and couldn't shake it. The way Gunnar couldn't. Rage climbed up his spine. Exploding into action, Gunnar kicked the coffee table over, sending the coffee cups Liam and he had left the other morning flying. He'd been too busy to carry them to the sink. Now, one was missing a handle. Gunnar stared at it. The back of his throat burned. He was good at breaking things.

Liam's expression, as Gunnar had made his accusation, flared to life in Gunnar's mind. He'd been hurt and confused by Gunnar's mistrust. All this time they'd been together with Liam being perfect, and Gunnar couldn't shake Boston's bullshit. Boston's claims weren't true. Gunnar knew it in his heart. Liam was this amazing man who'd given Gunnar hope in the face of a pointless future. Boston was a monster who drained the life from everyone he encountered. Why did he always let Boston destroy him?

Taking up his post on the couch, Gunnar opened the blinds and focused on Kaz's car. The moment the man left Liam alone, he'd go upstairs and throw himself at Liam's feet. Fuck. He really didn't know if that would be enough.

LIAM STOOD UNDER THE STREAM OF scalding water until it ran ice cold. Even then, it took his brain a minute to absorb the discomfort. All along he'd felt something off with Boston. He hadn't been able to put his finger on it. Mostly, it was due to where they'd met, but the doubt had been there. Now there were so many questions—terrible doubts—running through his mind.

He shoved his legs inside his sweat pants without drying off. It wasn't intentional. He was simply broken. Had Boston slit his tires? He'd thought there'd been something strange about Boston's timing. Liam fell face down on the bed and buried his head beneath the pillow. The bed shifted beside him. Liam peeked out from underneath the pillow. Kaz rolled onto his side and met Liam's stare. His eyes were turning black, making the jade of Kaz's irises shine even brighter. Somehow, Liam was to blame for this. Everything was always his fault.

"Are you okay?"

Kaz shrugged in way of answer. "It's hardly the first time I've taken a hit."

Liam's hand moved before he thought things through. He linked fingers with Kaz and squeezed.

"I'm so sorry."

A bemused look crossed Kaz's features. "For what?"

It was Liam's turn to shrug. "For having shit judgment, I suppose. I knew Gunnar would hurt me, but still I didn't stay away. When Boston started coming around, I felt it in my gut something wasn't right, but I didn't say anything to anyone."

One corner of Kaz's mouth lifted. "I suppose if your taste in people is shit, I'm also on that list."

With a groan, Liam ducked beneath the pillow once more. The thick cotton material did nothing to drown out Kaz's chuckle. Liam couldn't find the humor because Kaz was right. If he was being honest with himself, that was the real reason he'd ignored the inner voice, warning him something wasn't quite right with Boston. Other than Gunnar and Kaz, both of which had been in Liam's bed, Liam didn't have any real friends. Sometimes he craved the insight of someone he hadn't slept with. Kaz had a ton of friends. Gunnar traveled quite a bit. Liam was just alone.

Kaz pulled the pillow off Liam's head and threw it off the bed. His gaze moved over Liam's face, leaving Liam no choice but to accept Kaz's perusal or turn away. "Talk to me."

Liam swallowed. He really didn't want to. When the silence stretched on a moment too long, a flash of hurt passed over Kaz's face, and the confession fell without Liam's permission. "I can't stay here." He didn't know why he was whispering, but he couldn't make his voice louder no matter how hard he tried. The understanding in Kaz's expression had Liam repeating himself. "I can't stay here, knowing he's right beneath me, hating me. Kaz, I can't do this."

"I'm saying this even after that fucker hit me in my face, but Boston wasn't wrong. You don't need to feel guilty, and you shouldn't let Gunnar's insecurities run you from your home."

In spite of everything Kaz said, and to his horror, a tear slid from the corner of his eye. "Gunnar's not wrong either. I am."

Kaz's eyes narrowed. His temper made an appearance. "That's such bullshit, Liam. It pisses me off to no end that you'd allow anyone to make you cry. You're such a good person, and you surround yourself with shit, and yes, that includes me." He leapt from the bed and headed for the closet. He threw the door open with enough force it bounced off the wall and would've closed again if Kaz hadn't been standing in the way. His rage had Liam sitting up.

"What are you doing?"

Kaz snagged two shirts off hangers violently enough to send the hangers flying. "What's it fucking look like? I'm packing you a goddamn bag."

Liam swiped at his eyes. He hated when Kaz was angry. It didn't happen often, but it was ugly when it did. "Why are you packing me a bag?"

The annoyed look Kaz shot over his shoulder might've made Liam laugh if he wasn't dying inside from the hatred he'd seen in Gunnar's eyes. "You said you can't stay here, and your car is still at the tire shop. So I'm doing what I should've done a long fucking time ago. I'm taking care of you. You're coming home with me."

"Kaz," Liam began.

Kaz turned on him. "Anything you have to say to me while using that regretful tone, you can keep to your goddamn self. This isn't about me, and it has nothing to do with what I said in the car earlier. I know you're in love with Gunnar. There's nothing I can do or say that'll ever fix what I broke. This is about our friendship, which can't be broken, by the way. You need me, and I'm here, so get your fucking shit to-gether, and let me help you."

Funnily enough, Kaz's rage was exactly what Liam needed. He hurt too badly to feel any fury in his own defense. A giant ball of orange fur landed on Liam's leg. Kaz's expression went from enraged to confused.

"When did you get a cat?"

Liam bit the inside of his cheek to keep from smiling as he ran his fingers through Loki's fur. He must've followed Liam upstairs. Liam had been too upset to notice. "Today, I guess."

Kaz's confusion transformed into resignation. "I guess I'm taking a cat home with me too."

"It would seem so," Liam said without an ounce of regret.

"Fuck me," Kaz said with a heavy sigh, but Liam knew Kaz would let him have his way.

## Chapter Nine

"GODDAMN, Gunnar. We need to hang out more often outside the gym. You've got some sexy as fuck friends."

At Aden's bellowed claim, Gunnar turned away from his sparring partner. Kaz stood shoulder to shoulder with Aden. The groan building in Gunnar's head competed with marveling over Kaz's expression. He didn't look annoyed, embarrassed, or impressed with Aden's compliment. His face was blank, except his eyes. Kaz's gaze burned with barely suppressed hatred. It was aimed at Gunnar.

With an inner sigh, Gunnar dipped between the ropes. As he passed Aden, the gigantic trainer's tone changed, hardening.

"You're on the fecking clock, Gunnar. This place isn't a conversation parlor."

Gunnar dipped his chin, understanding Aden's frustration. "Got it."

"I hope so. Your head's not in this—like it should be if you're fighting Boston."

"It's on me," Kaz said behind them, dragging Aden's gaze his way.

Aden winked and walked away without further lecture. Gunnar couldn't bring himself to greet Kaz. This man had taken Liam away without giving Gunnar a chance to explain. This man loved the man of Gunnar's dreams. Rage wasn't a strong enough word to describe how Gunnar felt.

"How did you find me?"

Kaz's face screwed up in confusion at Gunnar's question. "Why? Are you in the witness protection program? I went by your apartment and you weren't there. This was the next logical place."

That made sense, and Gunnar felt a bit like a jackass. "I guess what I really meant was, why did you come looking for me in the first place?"

Instead of answering Gunnar's question, Kaz went for Gunnar's throat. "Every day, I wake up, and the first thought I have is of Liam." Kaz said the words as if ripping off a bandage and with no mercy in his heart.

Gunnar tilted his chin up, praying for intervention. He'd wondered how deep Kaz's feelings for Liam still ran. Now, he knew. "I don't want to hear this."

"I don't give a shit what you want," Kaz said, refusing to take pity on him. "You're going to hear this, because if you don't, it won't be long before you're me. Trust me, you don't want that. You don't want to wake up every day with your heart choosing someone who gets up every day choosing someone else. It will happen. Liam will move on. He won't mourn you forever or sit around waiting for you to figure out you're a dumbass."

"You're skating on thin ice with the dumbass comments."

Kaz ignored him. "Liam excels in every way, but one—forgiveness. Sure, he lets shit go, and eventually he might even stay friends with you. But once his love dies, you're out. His heart locks up like an uncrackable safe. He will never let you in again. Have you really considered that?"

He had, but damned if Gunnar would admit it to someone who continuously called him a dumbass and was in love with Gunnar's man.

At Gunnar's silence, Kaz continued. "I don't think you have. Not really. If you have, take whatever hell you've envisioned and times it by a thousand. That's what it's like for me, knowing he loves you."

"Why are you here?" Gunnar ground out the question between clenched teeth, because not only could he envision such a hell, he fucking hated hearing someone else felt the same way about Liam. Liam belonged to Gunnar.

Kaz didn't pull any punches. "Because I love him more than I love myself," Kaz answered, sounding sad. It pulled at Gunnar's heartstrings, even though he didn't like it. "Liam deserves happiness, and for some fucked up reason, he's chosen you. If you're too stupid to reach for him, I need to know now, so I can be there for the fall."

Gunnar's jealousy came back with a vengeance. "Why? So you can slip right back inside his bed? I see what you're doing."

Kaz shook his head, refusing the bait. "So I can be the friend he needs rather than the one he wants. So I can help cut you right out of his heart, instead of feeding him a bunch of bull-shit hope that will only end up killing him."

Gunnar's gaze dropped to his toes. The last person he wanted to talk to about any of this was Kaz. It seemed there was no avoiding it. "I love him too much to give up on him. I'd planned to apologize yesterday after you left, but you took Liam with you. Then I tried catching him at work, but he didn't show."

"He doesn't want to stay above you with you hating him, so I took him home with me. He didn't go to work because he thinks what he does for a living contributed to you thinking him capable of cheating on you."

Gunnar winced. Liam needed a keeper if he thought something so ridiculous. "I could never hate him or think badly of him."

"Then what the fuck, dude?" Kaz asked, sounding angry for the first time.

No matter how hard he tried, Gunnar couldn't lift his gaze from his feet to focus on Kaz. "I'm so goddamn angry with myself. How can I ask Liam to forgive me for something even I don't understand? Boston, he's like a disease. He's a cancer I had to cut out of myself, because he grows and spreads, tainting everything he touches. Seeing him again, with Liam standing between us, it was..." Gunnar lifted his chin, meeting Kaz's stare, and the words tumbled out. "It was like I knew Boston wouldn't stop until Liam is dead. Not physically, but emotionally. You don't know Boston. He takes and drains, making you want it while hating him for it. I was celibate for two years after him because I had nothing left inside me, until Liam."

The shock on Kaz's face couldn't be missed, but he didn't let it hold him back. "Then why are you letting Boston take anything else from you? Trust Liam. The way he's trusted you. There's no one else like him. His heart is a bear trap. It doesn't let go, and if Boston tries getting in, he'll be the one gnawing off his own leg, hoping for an escape." Kaz took a step away and switched his attention Aden's way. He pointed at the huge Irishman. "Whiskey, straight up, right?"

A bellow reached Gunnar's ears, but he didn't turn to look. He was too lost in his worries.

"How'd you know?"

"I'm lucky that way," Kaz called across the room. "Come by Merge some time. I'll buy you a drink to make up for cutting into your training time."

"Aye. I'll take you up on that."

When Kaz focused on Gunnar again, his eyes shone with laughter.

Gunnar couldn't stop with the confessions. "Aden likes everyone better than me."

Kaz's smile grew. "Sort of like your cat."

A loud sigh escaped Gunnar. "Yeah, exactly like that."

"ARE YOU GOING TO WORK TONIGHT OR ARE we staying in again?"

A spurt of guilt hit Liam at Kaz's question. "You don't have to stay home with me. I know you need the money."

The annoyed look crossing Kaz's features said a lot about how he felt about Liam's claim. "Don't be an ass. Of course I have to stay home if you do. It's your time of need and all that."

"It'll be your time of need if you keep missing work," Liam grumbled under his breath. "Plus, I'll be fine alone. You left me alone this morning, and I was still kicking when you got home."

"Damn," Kaz grumbled, heading for the kitchen. "I thought you were asleep and wouldn't miss me."

Liam growled. "I'm not broken. You can leave me alone for a little while." He followed on

Kaz's heels, determined to be a pest until Kaz got over whatever overprotective kick he was on.

Kaz pulled a beer from the fridge before kicking the door closed behind him. He twisted off the cap, eyeing Liam in a way Liam hated—like Kaz thought Liam was weak. "I'll think about it." He turned the beer up, tossing back half of it before coming up for air. "Oh, look. I've had too much to drink to drive. Guess I have to stay home with you."

Tilting his chin up to the sky, Liam prayed for strength. "You're making me think I should go home. I'm disrupting your life."

Setting the bottle aside, Kaz moved to close the distance between them. Before Liam guessed at his intentions, Kaz wrapped one arm around Liam's waist and pressed his lips to Liam's temple. For a full minute, neither of them moved. Kaz felt like a friend for the first time in a long time. Closing his eyes, Liam absorbed the sensation.

"You are not a disruption," Kaz said against his skin. "You're a much needed vacation."

"Thanks for that."

Before Kaz could respond, someone knocked on the front door, pulling him away. As if tied to the man by an invisible string, Liam continued following in Kaz's path. When he realized what he was doing, he froze in the center of the living room, feeling like a lost puppy.

Kaz checked the peephole. Whatever he saw on the other side seemed to throw him for a loop. He backed away for a second before looking again as if the result would change.

"Who is it?" For some dumbass reason, Liam whispered the question as if they needed to hide from an evangelist.

Instead of answering, Kaz opened the door and stepped back, silently allowing the visitor inside. To Liam's horror, Boston breezed inside.

"Oh my God," Liam said, incapable of holding back his anger over Boston's presence. "Are you being serious right now? Why are you here? How did you even find me?"

"You didn't show up at work last night. The guys you work with have big mouths." Boston held his hands out as if beseeching Liam to hear him out. "Can we talk? That's it. Just talk."

"Why?" Liam couldn't hide his consternation. This guy had cost him everything, and here he was, asking for more. "What could you possibly have to say to me?" From the corner of his eye, Liam could see Kaz attempting to make himself invisible. Thankfully, he didn't leave them alone. Liam wasn't afraid of Boston. He was scared what he might do to Boston.

"I wanted to check on you and say I'm sorry. When I went to see Gunnar yesterday, I didn't think you'd be there. None of that was supposed to happen. It wasn't about you." Boston lowered his hands. "Come on, Liam. You know there's no way I could've planned all of that."

Instead of being mollified, Liam's rage kicked up a degree. "Then what were your intentions? They weren't innocent. I don't believe for one second we met by accident."

One corner of Boston's mouth lifted in rueful smile. "You don't want me to answer that."

"Yes. I do," Liam said, eyebrows raised and not bothering to hide his animosity. "There's nothing you can say to me that'll make me hate you more than I do right now, so you might as well try for a bit of redemption."

Boston winced, but gave in. "I'd fully intended for Gunnar to see you leaving with me the night we met. He has a jealous streak a mile wide. I knew the moment he saw us together, he'd finally accept my challenge."

"But I didn't fall at your feet," Liam supplied, wondering if he could rip Boston's throat out before the man slung him off like a rabid dog.

Boston shook his head. "There's that, but also, I met you. You weren't what I expected." A small smile touched Boston's lips, softening his features. "I watched you for a while before approaching you. You're really ridiculous, you know that?"

Fuck, this guy. He'd ruined Liam's life and now he was calling Liam names. "Gee, thanks."

Boston snorted. "I didn't mean it as an insult. It's more that I don't get you. I sat there, watching you, and curiosity ate me alive. You turned down more money than you made and genuinely seemed happy to be talking with people who just wanted you to take your pants off. It's like you don't know your worth. Then we talked, and I made a terrible discovery. I like you. You're sexy and funny. The confidence you exude is enough to bowl any man over, but there's a vulnerable side to you that makes me want to corrupt you."

Liam was speechless, which was fine, since Boston wasn't finished.

"You also have a suspicious mind. I'm surprised you kept talking to me, but you did. People don't talk to me unless they want something. Not only would you not take my money, you gave me your name, even knowing it could cost your job. I was moved. As much as I need Gunnar to accept my challenge, for reasons all my own, I found myself wondering if I could do both—use you to force Gunnar's hand and steal you away."

Without question, Liam knew he'd never been more torn. A thousand responses raced to his tongue. They each died before passing his lips. A knock landed on the door, pulling Liam's focus away from trying to decide what he should do. Kaz glanced through the blinds.

"Oh, fuck. Gunnar's here."

Liam's shoulders fell. It was official. The universe hated him. If there had been any hope of him working things out with Gunnar, they were gone now. He cast a forlorn glance Kaz's way, seeking guidance. Kaz's features hardened into a determined expression.

Kaz snagged Boston's elbow. "You, move over here for half a second." A bemused expression crossed Boston's features, but he let Kaz urge him out of sight. Once Kaz had Boston situated, he snagged Liam's elbow and hauled him toward the door. "Keep your gaze averted from where Boston's car is, and Gunnar isn't likely to notice it. It's a pretty generic rental. Now, keep an open mind." With that last bit of advice hanging between them, Kaz opened the front door just enough where only Liam could be seen.

Liam's outrage over being forced to deal with Gunnar died away the second he set eyes on him. He swore the sun shone brighter while reflecting off Gunnar's eyes. Everything about

Gunnar, from the dip in the center of his chin to his sexy muscular jaw, was perfection. Love choked Liam, keeping his tongue glued to the roof of his mouth.

"You stole my cat," Gunnar said as way of greeting.

Liam chewed on his bottom lip, trying not to laugh at Gunnar's dry tone. "Your cat ran away."

"Seems he's not the only one," Gunnar said, twirling his finger at their surroundings and pointing out the obvious.

Liam's eyebrows rose against his will. "I came to stay with a friend during my time of need. That's hardly running away."

"Loki could probably say the same, but it doesn't change the fact neither of you are where you belong."

A hint of irritation creeped in, joining Liam's hurt over seeing Gunnar for the first time since their blowout. "If you want to take Loki back home with you, I can't stop you. He is your cat. But you don't get to decide where I should be."

Instead of lashing out, as Liam expected, Gunnar blew out a sigh. "No. You can bring Loki home when you decide it's where you belong as well."

Liam growled. He couldn't stop it from happening. "You don't want some cheating bastard, remember?"

"You're right. I don't. That's why I dumped Boston back when I caught him in bed with a welterweight fighter who was supposed to be my best friend."

*Ouch.* That hit Liam in the chest and made him immediately hate Boston even more than he already did. It also took every ounce of Liam's self-control to keep from glancing over his shoulder and giving Boston his death stare.

"I'm sorry if that's left me bitter," Gunnar said, saving Liam from giving away the fact that Boston was standing only feet away. "I'm doubly sorry if that means you're the one who's paying for his bullshit. You're who I want to spend the rest of my life with, and you're also my best friend. Seeing Boston again and hearing him talk as if the two of you had something going on, it was as if I was losing everything all over again. I don't expect you to grab your things and rush back home, but I also can't sit back and do nothing, expecting you'll simply forgive me one day. You mean everything to me."

A shove came from behind, pushing Liam out the door.

"This is because I love you," Kaz said as the door slammed behind Liam. The loud click of the lock turning couldn't be mistaken for anything else. Liam glanced down at his bare feet. Not only did he not have shoes, his phone and keys were inside as well. He was helpless.

"Well, this feels hauntingly familiar."

The door flew open, and Loki was shoved outside with a definite lack of grace. "This is because I care," Kaz added, slamming the door closed and locking it once more.

Liam watched Loki give an outraged flick of his tail before collapsing on top of Liam's feet as if nothing happened. Liam sighed. "It's like I'm always at your mercy."

Gunnar cupped Liam's chin, leaving him no other choice than to meet his gaze. There wasn't an ounce of triumph on Gunnar's face. He shook his head, denying Liam's claim.

"I'm at yours. If you tell me to take you home and never darken your door again, that's what I'll do. But I'm begging you to make my home yours, and never leave again, because I'm empty without you. Somewhere along the line, I went from being scared to love again to picturing Willa and Dakota as the cutest and most foul-mouthed flower girls in history. I miss holding you at night, waiting for you to fall asleep so I can whisper how much I love you."

The backs of Liam's eyes burned. "Do you do that?"

Gunnar's eyes were sad as he nodded.

Liam hated the thought of Gunnar ever being unhappy. "Why do you wait until I'm asleep?"

Taking a step closer, Gunnar wrapped his arms around Liam's waist, towing Liam against him. Loki hissed in protest. Gunnar ignored him. "The words are always hovering on my tongue. Every time I look at you, they're screaming in my head, but I didn't want to give you just words. You deserve actions. Anyone can tell you they love you. I wanted you to feel me, not hear me. You're so capable and independent. Nothing I thought to say or do ever felt like enough."

On the heels of Boston saying Liam was ridiculous and in obvious need of rescue, Gunnar was twice as amazing. No one else saw him the way Gunnar did. That was why he couldn't have a single lie or secret between them.

"Boston is inside. He got here like five minutes ahead of you. He came to apologize."

Gunnar's expression never changed. His gaze didn't waver. "I don't care what Boston says, does, or where he goes. Which is what I should've said yesterday. I know you. Better still, I trust you. Do I think he's still trying to pull some shit and isn't sorry about a single fucking thing? Yes, but that has nothing to do with us." Gunnar's fingers found their way beneath the back of Liam's shirt. He stroked Liam's spine. "Can we go home now? Loki's using my leg as a scratching post."

Backing up a step, Liam bent at the waist and snagged Loki before he did any more damage. As always, the moment Liam had him, Loki went limp, playing dead. With Loki draped over one arm, Liam grabbed a handful of Gunnar's shirt with his free hand and towed him forward. "Before we go, I have something I need to say too." Gunnar looked worried. Liam didn't want that. "I love you," he admitted before Gunnar let any negative thoughts sink in. "I shouldn't have let not saying it go on. As much as I want you to feel it too, I need to be saying it, and would've loved to have heard the words from you."

Gunnar captured his mouth, stealing Liam's thoughts and worries away. They'd be fine. He loved this man. Nothing would come between them, except Loki, whose weight increased as he tried pushing them apart. Liam pulled away, absorbing the flush on Gunnar's cheeks.

"When we get home, I'm locking your cat in the bathroom and having my way with you."

At Gunnar's claim, a huge grin pulled at the corners of Liam's mouth. "Awww, you called him mine."

"As if there was ever any doubt," Gunnar said, urging Liam toward the truck. "He adopted you the moment you stole me."

---

KAZ KEPT HIS FOREHEAD PRESSED TO THE door, absorbing every word spoken on the other side. Boston moved around behind him, doing something in Kaz's kitchen. The brief moments Kaz glanced behind him, it looked like Boston was searching Kaz's cabinets. Kaz couldn't work up a care beyond Boston making too much noise for Kaz to hear every word passing between Liam and Gunnar. When he felt a tug at the belt loop of his jeans, Kaz glanced over his shoulder, annoyed.

Boston tilted his chin toward the kitchen. "Come on. Listening to every word won't change the outcome."

Giving in, Kaz let Boston drag him to the kitchen. Boston snagged a chair from the dining room table as they went. He dropped it next to the counter before urging Kaz to sit.

Even as Kaz did as Boston bade, he protested. "You know this is my house, right?" Without waiting for Boston's answer, he added, "What are you doing anyhow?"

Boston rolled his eyes and picked up a Ziploc filled with ice. "I plan to question you about your Lord and Savior, Jesus Christ. What the fuck does it look like I'm doing?" He pressed the ice pack to worst part of Kaz's bruising. "You haven't been icing this or it wouldn't look this bad."

Kaz let it go on because he honestly didn't know how else to react. "It wouldn't look like this at all if you hadn't hit me," Kaz said, pointing out the obvious.

Boston's annoyed expression fell away, leaving his features blank and killing any chance Kaz had at reading the dude. Silence dragged out between them. With his one good eye—the one Boston didn't have covered in plastic and ice—Kaz stared at Boston. He could see where Gunnar had been coming from. Gunnar had said the man was poison, tainting everything, while making the person he ruined want it. Kaz could see Boston doing exactly that. Boston was beautiful. There was no other way to describe him. He equaled Kaz in height, but with sleeker muscles—like a finely tuned machine. In this case, a weapon. The man was the cruiserweight champion. That was huge, and it was also enough to leave a man star struck without Boston's overwhelming good looks. His blond hair and blue eyes were the perfect shade. Yeah, Kaz could see this man easily destroying someone's heart. The thing was, Boston also had some hidden agenda Kaz didn't get and probably never would.

"Why did you let me hit you?"

Boston's question pulled Kaz from cataloging every detail of him. "Who says I did?"

The smirk pulling at Boston's lips was enough to make Kaz want to wipe it away. "I'm a professional fighter. You let me hit you."

Boston shifted the ice pack slightly and Kaz closed both eyes, thankful for the reprieve. Tilting his chin up, Kaz gave himself over to Boston's care. He wasn't sure why Boston was doing this, but Kaz let it happen. Anything he could focus on besides what was happening outside his front door was a blessing. Anything at all. A pain hit Kaz in the center of his chest. Between his inability to breathe properly and the silent strength of Boston's ministrations, the confession fell from Kaz's lips without his permission.

"Maybe I wanted to hurt on the outside as badly as I do on the inside." As soon as the admission left Kaz's mouth, he wanted to take it back, especially in the silence that followed.

When Boston finally spoke, his tone changed from the all-business person who'd been caring for Kaz's injury to dark and tempting. "Maybe I could help you with that."

Kaz pushed the ice pack away and met Boston's gaze. He needed to know if the same sexual promise dripping from Boston's lips showed in his eyes. It did. "How do you plan to help me?"

A slow, wicked, and practiced smile pulled at Boston's lips. "Tell me how you want it, and I promise to make it hurt."

AFTER PULLING UP TO THE FRONT DOOR OF their apartment, Gunnar snagged Loki from Liam's lap. "Stay here for a second. I'll be right back," Gunnar said, stopping Liam from exiting the car. Liam's eyebrows rose in question, but he gave Gunnar a nod, letting him know he'd do as Gunnar asked. Gunnar ignored the way Loki's claws dug into his arm as he carried him through the door. With a quick apology, Gunnar set Loki inside and quickly shut the door again before he could escape. When he made it back to the truck, Liam eyed him with open curiosity as he rearranged a few things in and around the console. He shoved it up and out of the way before patting the now empty spot beside him.

"Come here. I have one more place to go and I want to hold you."

At Gunnar's demand, Liam dutifully un-snapped his seat belt and slid over. Once Gunnar had Liam where he wanted him, he dug around between the seats until he found the flimsy center-seat seat belt, and snapped it around Liam's waist. Personally, Gunnar had always thought the crap seat belts offered to whoever got stuck sitting in the middle was a joke. Still, there was no way in hell he was taking off without Liam belted in some manner. The man was too important. Liam let it happen without a single protest. The trust Liam always showed in him was humbling. Even though Gunnar hadn't given Liam a single clue as to where he was taking him, Liam didn't seem to care. Gunnar couldn't let it pass without comment.

"You haven't asked a single question."

Liam's fingers brushed Gunnar's jaw, pulling his gaze away from Liam's seat belt to Liam's eyes. There was so much love staring at him, Gunnar could barely breathe. "I just want to be with you. Nothing else matters."

Dipping his chin, Gunnar placed a light kiss on Liam's palm. "I have something I want to show you real quick. Don't worry. I haven't forgotten you don't have any shoes. You won't need them for this."

"I'm not worried," Liam said without hesitation. "You always take care of me."

Gunnar put the truck in reverse. "That hasn't always been true. I failed you yesterday and the night before that. But I swear, I'll never disappoint you again. That's why I need to show you something."

Liam's palm slid up Gunnar's leg as they headed out. Only the sure knowledge they would wreck if he couldn't see kept Gunnar's eyes from falling closed at the contact. Liam's touch got better every time. To keep his sanity, Gunnar explained his reasoning as he drove.

"Back when you were a sophomore and I was a junior, we had wildlife management together for second period."

"We did?"

Gunnar chuckled at the disbelief in Liam's voice. "Yeah. I sat directly behind you."

"How did I miss that?"

Gunnar's jaw popped, and he had to call his temper under control before he answered. He'd forgotten how much he'd truly hated Liam's daily torment. His silent rage on Liam's behalf had manifested itself Gunnar's senior year into an explosion of fury that had almost ended in his expulsion. If he hadn't been the football team's star player, he would've been out on his ass after nearly breaking that one dude's arm. Liam had been worth it.

"You always had your head down," Gunnar answered, hating bringing up the hard times, but needing to get this off his chest. "The worst of your tormentors were in that class. You always looked at your shoes coming and going the whole year. All throughout class, you stared at the top of your desk." Swallowing down his anger over that, Gunnar concentrated on the good memories. "While you were looking at everything but the people around you, I didn't see anything or anyone but you."

Gunnar turned onto the road leading to Crocodile Lake and continued his story. "Then, one day, we went on a field trip to Crocodile Lake."

Liam chuckled. It was such a sexy sound. Gunnar's muscles tensed, longing. "I remember that. The guy leading the tour plucked me out of line and forced me to hold a snake."

Gunnar nodded. "I know. I was standing a foot away from you at the time. From the moment we stepped off the bus, I followed on your heels, keeping tabs on your every move. You were wearing a blue shirt that matched your eyes, and you smelled sinful. That guide snagged you out of line because he'd been eyeing you like a fucking candy bar the entire tour."

"No way," Liam said, interrupting him.

Gunnar traced an X across his chest. "Cross my heart. I half expected the perv to lick you at any moment. Anyhow, the look on your face was priceless when he shoved that snake in your hands. You glanced my way, biting your bottom lip and looking so unsure of yourself. I winked. Even I don't know why. It was like I was lending you strength."

"I don't remember that," Liam said, sounding slightly disbelieving.

Gunnar laughed. "This is all true. I swear. For me, it's like it happened yesterday," Gunnar added as he pulled into Crocodile Lake wildlife reserve and maneuvered his truck to the quiet spot he'd intended to take Liam to all those years ago. "When I winked, your expression changed. In an instant, you looked wicked as hell. You smirked. I just knew, in your head, you were telling me you were in control. In that moment, I knew, if I ever got you alone, you would rock my world." He put the truck in park and focused on Liam. "That's when the fantasy of having you in this place began. Every time I woke up covered in sweat, and other things, it was after dreaming about you and me—here."

Liam's tongue shot out, moistening his bottom lip before he looked away. His gaze moved over their surroundings, completely unware of the way Gunnar's cock leaked. All it had taken was watching the simple act of Liam licking his lip, and Gunnar was a goner.

"So that's why you invited me here that night you met me after work?"

Gunnar nodded.

A line appeared between Liam's brows. "I don't understand. Why didn't you argue your case or try calling me after that night?"

Gunnar felt the rueful smile pull at his lips. He was helpless against it. "Because I was a stupid teenager. You'd rejected my big fantasy. Last night, I realized I was making the same mistake twice. Back then, you didn't realize you were important to me because you're not a mind reader. The same thing applies now. I didn't tell you back then I expected we'd end up together. This time around, I wasn't telling you that I expected you would eventually marry me. So, here we are at the intersection of my old fantasy and my new one. I didn't plan this ahead of time. It'll probably look like a shit effort to you, but will you marry me?"

Liam's expression didn't change as he answered, "Yes."

At Liam's less-than-enthusiastic response, Gunnar felt moved to point out the obvious. "You don't look happy."

Liam nodded, even as his expression still didn't budge. "Inside my head, I'm squealing like a group of tween girls at their first boy-band concert. It's an unattractive picture. I'm trying to stop it from becoming reality."

With every word Liam spoke, Gunnar's smile grew. Now Liam had put the image in his head, he could picture Liam doing just that, and he wanted it, but it was obvious Liam didn't. "Is there a happy medium between tween girls and the attending a funeral face you're giving me now?"

A smile exploded across Liam's face. He ripped off his seat belt and straddled Gunnar's hips. "Will this do?" Liam asked before covering Gunnar's mouth with his. As Liam's delicious flavor coated his taste buds, Gunnar wondered if a person could actually explode from an overload of happiness. He feared he was in danger of finding out. Liam filled every dark place inside him. Gunnar's bouts of depression had completely disappeared since they'd started dating. Liam had transformed Gunnar's life.

Reaching between them, Gunnar shaped Liam's erection through his shorts, wondering if he could make the man come by teasing alone. He loved when Liam's cum covered his skin. In those moments, Liam made him feel powerful enough to take over the world. The sting of Liam's teeth sinking into Gunnar's bottom lip had Gunnar's pulse beating in his ears. The sound of blood rushing through his veins, on the way to his erection, almost drowned out the sound of knocking on the driver's side window.

Liam jerked away. The flush on the other man's cheeks could've been embarrassment or lust. Either way, it was sexy as hell and Gunnar had a hard time tearing his gaze away to focus on their intruder. When he caught sight of the same cop who'd almost busted them last time, Gunnar lowered the window, praying the autograph he'd given last time would sustain him.

"How's it going this evening, Mr. Samson? You still having trouble out of that check engine light?"

To his horror, heat exploded across Gunnar's face. He had to clear his throat to speak. "Um, not this time. It was..." Gunnar trailed off, incapable of thinking of a single excuse.

Liam kept his face averted. The flush didn't lessen. Now, Liam also shook with barely suppressed laughter. The sensation did nothing to help with Gunnar's erection.

"I think I see what it was. Is there a reason your..."

"My fiancé, Liam," Gunnar supplied when it became obvious the cop didn't know how to describe Liam.

He gave Gunnar a sharp nod. "Is there a reason your fiancé is wearing the same horrified expression today as he was the last time we spoke?"

Seeing nothing for it, Gunnar went for the bare minimum of truth. "Probably because I propositioned him on the side of the road that night too," Gunnar said, taking the full blame without an ounce of shame. "It's all me. I'm easily the luckiest man alive and can't keep my hands to myself when Liam's around." By the time Gunnar finished, the policeman wore a bright smile.

He leaned an elbow against Gunnar's open window, as if Liam wasn't still straddling Gunnar's hips, and they were there for a visit. "I'm hoping by how happy you sound your fans will finally get to see you go after that cruiserweight championship. It's been a real shame, watching that Boston bastard hold on to the title."

Gunnar nodded, seeing a way out of this mess. "Yes, sir. The official announcement hasn't gone out yet, but a challenge match has been set for three months from now in Vegas. If you've got a card with your info on it, I'll make sure you get a couple of tickets."

With a tap of his knuckles on Gunnar's door, the cop leaned away. "That's excellent news." He handed Gunnar a card with his info. "My wife will be thrilled to hear it."

"Great," Gunnar said, hoping he got to be alone with Liam sometime tonight. He cast a quick glance at the card, noting the man's name was David. "Maybe I'll get to meet your wife in Vegas."

"She'd love that, I'm sure," David said. "Now, my rounds bring me back this way in about two hours. I expect I won't find you here by then."

"Sure thing," Gunnar agreed. With a final wave, Gunnar watched David in his side view mirror until the man pulled away. When he met Liam's stare, Liam's gaze shone with humor. "Sounds like I have a little over an hour to make those teenage fantasies come true. Where should I start?"

Gunnar tapped his lips. "Right here. You've already made every other fantasy come true."

Liam moved closer, wrapping his arms around Gunnar's neck. He stared at Gunnar's mouth. Gunnar massaged Liam's nape, hoping to convince him to close the final gap between them. He loved the way Liam tasted.

Liam didn't let Gunnar have his way. "How exactly have I made your fantasies come true? I've barely touched you."

Gunnar didn't hesitate. "You said yes."

"Ooh, you're good."

Gunnar chuckled and nipped at Liam's bottom lip. "Yes. I am. Let me prove it."

And he did. For two days, Gunnar wouldn't let Liam leave his bed. When they were together, good didn't begin to cover it.

# Chapter Ten

SIX MONTHS of training and fretting came down to this—a single night of glory or complete failure. Gunnar could barely hear his thoughts over the noise of the crowd. Every new move he'd practiced flew out the window. Loud music filled his ears. An eerie silence fell, making the chords sound that much louder. It seemed Gunnar should've been nervous before now. Everything up until this point felt completely right. This was the first time—with everyone's eyes upon him—Gunnar questioned if he would fail.

Liam's scent filled his nostrils. Gunnar automatically pulled him closer and made the first move, leading them out for their first dance as a married couple. Once he had Liam in his arms, it didn't matter who looked on or if he missed a step. It was equally unimportant that he hadn't a single dance lesson before planning their wedding. All that mattered was the man in his arms.

"I love you." The words fell so easily from Gunnar's lips. Liam's smile made him want to say it again.

"I love you too."

"When do I get to have you alone?" Liam's laughter at Gunnar's question filled Gunnar to the brim. He really wanted an answer, but Dakota pushed her way between them, claiming Gunnar as her dance partner before Liam responded.

She tried dancing on his toes, but even then she was too short. Giving up, Gunnar swept her into his arms. He hugged her to his chest and tossed the steps out the window in exchange for having fun. His gaze moved to Liam. He had Willa in his arms, doing the same. Their eyes met and held. One day, Gunnar hoped they'd have children of their own. For now, they enjoyed having their nights alone.

Sometimes Gunnar would think about his life and marvel how it was nothing more than a series of circles, always leading him back to the same places. He'd started out secretly obsessed with the too-brave boy down the street and ended up marrying that same sexy man after finding out he lived above him. At one time, he'd craved being the best in his weight class only to give up the dream to his ex. He'd easily stripped that title away for himself three months ago after life had circled back around again.

All the times he'd turned down Boston's challenges, Gunnar hadn't realized how much he had to gain by winning. He made enough money so that Liam didn't have to work a job he hated, and Gunnar didn't have to keep traveling for fights. Once that realization stepped in, Gunnar had worked his ass off to gain that title. There was nothing he wouldn't do for a better life with Liam.

Spotting Dakota's dad, Mike, Gunnar passed her over and reclaimed his husband. He needed Liam's sweet flavor coating his tongue and the warmth of Liam's skin against his. Gunnar's lungs didn't work properly again until he had it. Gunnar pressed his lips to the shell of Liam's ear.

"Sometimes you terrify me," Gunnar admitted. "I see the way every eye follows you, and I wonder if you'll get bored with me one of these days."

A snort left Liam, warming Gunnar's heart. "Hush, idiot. You've already clinched this deal.

If you need convincing of how awesome you are, wait until we're alone. I'll fall on my knees and worship you the way you deserve."

That was all Gunnar needed to hear. His life was complete.

# About the Author

Charity Parkerson is an award winning and multi-published author with several companies. Born with no filter from her brain to her mouth, she decided to take this odd quirk and insert it in her characters.

*2015 Readers' Favorite Award Winner

*Winner of 2, 2014 Readers' Favorite Awards

*2015 Passionate Plume Award Finalist

*2013 Readers' Favorite Award Winner

*2013 Reviewers' Choice Award Winner

*2012 ARRA Finalist for Favorite Paranormal Romance

\*Five-time winner of The Mistress of the Darkpath